Wicked Game

Mercy Celeste

Copyright © 2014 Mercy Celeste

All rights reserved.

ISBN: **1499289499**
ISBN-13: **978-1499289497**

Copyright

Wicked Game is a work of fiction. Names, characters, places, and incidents are the product of the author's imagination or are used fictitiously. Any resemblance to actual persons, living or dead, events, or locales is entirely coincidental.

Copyright © 2014 by Mercy Celeste

All rights reserved.

Published in the United States by Mercy Celeste

Warning: All rights reserved. No part of this book may be reproduced in any many without written permission, except for brief quotations embodied in critical articles and reviews.

Contact the publisher for further information:

mercyceleste@gmail.com

Mercy Celeste

Wicked Game

Acknowledgements

Cover Art provided by
Reece Notley

Mercy Celeste

Wicked Game

Dedication

I'd like to take a moment and thank Liquid Silver Books who originally published Wicked Game and Double Coverage. Thank you for giving me a chance.

And I'd like to say that I wrote this book in November, 2010 for the NaNoWriMo project. I wrote the entire first draft in that month. I had planned to update the manuscript for rerelease but while reading I realized that if I tried to bring the story into the world of 2014 I'd have to rewrite significant parts of it due to new rules in football. And it would be a shame to not have the on field phone sex scene now. So this book is set in the original time period of circa 2009 with the rules as I knew them to be and all pop culture references of the time. I have changed nothing. This is the same story it was before.

And to the fans who stick with me I'd like to say thank you. From the very bottom of my heart.

Mercy

Mercy Celeste

WICKED GAME

Mercy Celeste

Chapter One

Tuscaloosa, Alabama
Spring, 2009

Some days it just did not pay to get out of bed. Today was one of those days. Cass Pendleton, recently unemployed schoolteacher, stood at the door the temp agency sent her to, biting her bottom lip in indecision.

On the one hand, she had bills to pay, and that ever-present need to eat something daily demanded she find a job. After six months of part-time, then substitute jobs, her savings had run out.

On the other, boxed mac and cheese somehow didn't sound so bad, she decided as she stared at the name on the door. Why did it have to be him, of all people?

Jamison Dalton.

With any luck, the boy she went to school with would not be sitting behind that door.

If there was ever a God in heaven, there would a nice older man sitting in that office, who just happened to have the same name as her childhood nemesis.

"Come in." The voice that came through the door at her knock was deep. Deeper than Jaime's had been the last time she'd seen him. Probably his dad. God, please let it be his dad. Jamison Senior. What exactly had Jaime's dad done for a living?

He was an accountant, check. Accounting office? Check. Things were looking up.

Uncheck. Jaime's dad had died in a car accident their senior year. Oh, shit. She closed her eyes, and with one last prayer of hope going up to the heavens, pushed the door open.

He was a big man, tall with broad shoulders that looked as if he should be wrestling on cable television. Brutally handsome—but then he always had been, even as far back as kindergarten. His hair was the only thing about him that was the same as she remembered.

Straight, not blond but not exactly brown either, with long unruly bangs that were always in his eyes. He was tan, as if he spent a great deal of time outdoors. Which considering his profession, he probably did.

"Who are you?" He didn't look at her; there was impatience in his voice as he riffled through papers on his desk. He'd always been impatient, nothing new there.

"Cassandra Pendleton. The nanny agency sent me to interview." Maybe he wouldn't remember her. She smoothed her skirt and shifted her weight from one low-heeled pump to the other, waiting for him to acknowledge her.

When he finally looked up at her, with eyes the color of smoldering bourbon, she lost her breath. Oh, effin' hell. Jaime had grown into an incredible specimen of manhood.

Skinny, runty Jaime Dalton was, in a word, breathtaking.

"I grew up with a girl by that same name." He looked her up and down, as if trying to find the chubby girl she'd once been beneath her clothes. "She was a damned annoying girl who used to hide my backpack at the bus stop. She also caused me to miss the bus a couple of times."

"That wasn't me and you know it, Jaime Dalton." Damn, she'd walked into that one nose first.

"It could have been Ginger Beasley or Kelvin Hughes now that I think about it." He placed his elbows on the desk and steepled his fingers in front of his face while he studied her. Those damned gold eyes sizing her up for the kill. "How have you been, Cass?"

"Pretty good. How about yourself?" Damn, but that sounded clumsy. But, he'd always made her feel like that. Stupid and fat and clumsy.

"Can't complain." He smiled a tight-lipped smile, more like a smirk, but she was being generous in her assessment. "You've come about the job? What are your qualifications?"

"Well, I graduated summa cum laude with a bachelor's degree in English and a minor in history. I earned my master's degree in early childhood education, and I am about halfway to my doctorate in child psychology. I taught for three years at a small private school in Tennessee before moving back here, where I took a teaching job in the public school system. My job, along with dozens more, went away last year due to budget cuts. I love children and can't envision myself ever working in a field without them." Cass quoted automatically. She knew every word by heart, but there was just no real way to make "laid off through no fault of my own" sound appealing. "I didn't know you had children. Sorry, I don't know why I just said that." Waiting for the red to infuse his face, she gulped. She knew from experience how quick tempered he could be, but it never came; instead, he smiled. "I don't." What?

"So you decided to call up the local nanny agency for what, then? Kicks?" His smile widened, becoming almost menacing, and Cass found herself taking a step back toward the door. Something was definitely off here.

"Well, Cass, I guess I'm busted." He leaned back in his chair, his hands caressing the armrests as he watched her. "The owner of the temp agency you are with is a friend of mine from college. She has helped me with staffing problems in the past. I thought I'd call her up and see if she had any semi-intelligent applicants who could actually read and write, not to mention type, with a pleasant speaking voice. Someone who isn't looking for a sugar daddy to put a rock on her finger."

"In other words, you need a secretary."

"A personal assistant."

"And my name came up?"

"I thought I'd died and gone to heaven when April sent me over a photo of you." His gaze caressed Cass's body in a way that sent shivers down her spine. "Damn, Cass, but you grew up in all the right places."

"And you're still an asshole."

"I'm a rich asshole, and I need an assistant to handle my business without trying to … er … handle my business, if you catch my meaning." The smoldering gaze he continued to sweep her with belied that statement. "And I want you."

"I'm sorry. I can think of about a thousand less potentially fatal things I'd rather do with my time, Mr. Dalton."

"I take that as a no, then." There should have been anger or disappointment in his eyes. She remembered all the times she'd thwarted his plans as children. The time she refused to play doctor with him at a neighbor's birthday party. The time he'd lost class president to her. The time — well, the times — his temper had gotten the best of him growing up, were too numerous to count. However, this time was different; this time the look that came into his eyes was more a look of triumph rather than a defeat.

"That would be correct." She pivoted on the ball of her foot and reached for the brass doorknob. "Good day."

"I'm prepared to double your teacher salary." She heard the confidence in his voice and imagined the triumph in his eyes reaching a burning point when she paused.

"Good day, Mr. Dalton."

"Okay, you've got me over a barrel. Ninety grand a year, Cass, and all you have to do is answer my phone, schedule my appointments, and keep the groupies at bay. Oh yeah, and be at my beck and call around the clock. Hell, I'll even throw in a car, major medical, and two weeks paid vacation anywhere you want to go." Her breath caught in her throat, choking her. She squeezed the door handle, determined to walk out with her back straight and her head held high. She wanted to hear disappointment in his voice when he called out to her, she wanted to hear him beg and plead and throw a temper tantrum when she wouldn't play nice.

She hated mac and cheese.

Damn. "When do I start?"

She hated that laugh. Spoiled rotten bloated egotistical … asshole.

"I leave for Miami in the morning. Be ready to go. No need to pack; you'll pick up something after we arrive."

"How long will we be in Miami?" She would have to find someone to water her plants and get the mail…

"Permanently. That's where I live. I hope that is not a problem." Yes, it was a problem. Crap.

"For the record, I still think you're an asshole."

"I wouldn't have it any other way, Cass." She could hear him grin. God damn him.

Goddamn Jaime Dalton all to hell. "I'll send a driver to your mother's house at seven in the morning. Don't keep him waiting."

And just like that, he dismissed her. Jaime Dalton had just rearranged her very life and dismissed her as if he were some sort of god who had the right to do with her as he pleased.

And she'd let him. Shit. Crap. She needed to reevaluate her loathing of mac and cheese.

Cass pushed the door open and walked briskly through the empty hallway of the quiet office building. She smiled at the receptionist at the front desk on her way past, as if she had not just sold her soul to her childhood nemesis.

* * * * *

The Cass Pendleton he remembered was a little shorter and definitely rounder in the hip area, flatter in the chest area. She kept her hair short and wore loose clothing to hide the weight she'd carried back then. Of course, he remembered her mouth and her ego as well as she apparently remembered his. She never had a confidence problem, despite her weight problem, and in fact gave better than she got.

In fact, as he let himself walk down memory lane, she'd been bound and determined to compete with him as much as he'd been determined to get her attention. And that had always been a problem for him. Cass had been the only girl in his life who hadn't wanted his attention. Even as far back as kindergarten, when they'd first met, she, for some reason, just did not like him. Okay, so maybe it had something to do with pulling her hair that first day. She had such pretty hair, brown and silky. He remembered wanting to know what it felt like; it wasn't his fault she snatched her head away, causing him to yank it instead.

Birthday parties, school functions, debate

team, it didn't matter; Cass was always there, always taunting him, always trying to one-up him. She'd made it her life's ambition in junior year to win class president just because he thought it might be fun.

Damn, but Cass had frustrated him. There was that one time at the Anderson twins' pool party, when a group of his teammates had thrown her into the pool fully dressed.

She'd come up sputtering and mad as a wet cat, and somehow she'd thought he'd been the mastermind. He could only remember her breasts when she attacked him, her white T-shirt and bra now transparent, molded to her body like a second skin. The things running through his head had embarrassed him, his body's reaction was unbearable, and he spent the rest of the party hiding in the pool house.

She was a first-class thorn not a rose, so why exactly did he jump at the chance to add her to his employ? Ninety grand a year wasn't going to hurt him. He couldn't help wondering if being around her now that she'd shed the baby fat and become a beauty would somehow be his own undoing. Whatever happened, he knew one thing for sure.

This was going to be one hell of a season.

Mercy Celeste

Chapter Two

They said that the best defense was a good offense. Cass packed her bags, being careful to include her most teacherly clothes. She didn't want Jamison Dalton getting the wrong idea right out of the gate. She wasn't a floozy. She had a brain and a reputation to protect. The last thing she wanted to deal with was Jamison Dalton being Jamison Dalton.

She pulled a stack of cardigans out of her dresser drawer and tucked them into the largest case. Would she even need cardigans in Miami, she wondered, or stockings or tights or even a jacket? Did it ever get cold in Miami? Exactly how long did Jamison live in Miami each year? She knew his career took him all over the country during the season.

Would she be required to travel with him to games, or just manage things from his Miami office?

"Damn!" Why had she let this happen to her—why? "Mom, what should I take? I've never been to Florida before, and Jaime didn't tell me anything."

"It's Miami, dear—pretty sundresses and a bikini or several bikinis. They don't wear that much down there. Sunscreen. Don't forget that." For some reason, there was a trill to her mother's voice, almost as if she were happy that her only child was picking up and leaving with no notice.

"You're a big help. Seriously, what do I need? And don't say sunscreen and a smile.

I doubt the sunscreen will make it past airport security, and I'm fresh out of smiles."

"Honey, just pack the things you'll miss if you leave them behind. Jaime said not to worry about clothes, didn't he? Then don't worry, he'll make sure you have everything you need. Nicer stuff than those ratty old cardigans. He has an image to uphold after all."

"Still not helping," Cass shouted down the hallway, but the sound of the doorbell sent her into a tizzy of emotions. "No, no, no, I'm not ready. It's not even seven yet. Aiiiii."

"Good morning. I presume you are here to whisk my daughter away to paradise?" she heard her mother say at the door.

"Still not helping." Her heart slammed into her chest wall, pounding harder as she looked around the room she'd spent her childhood in. She had everything she thought she might need, clothes, phone, iPod, and laptop. What was she forgetting? She grabbed a couple of old paperbacks off the bookshelf, to read on the plane, and the old bunny that sat in the middle of her bed, she couldn't leave Mr. Flop behind.

"Cass, you've got everything. Stop worrying and go start your new life." Her mom stood in the doorway, her eyes shimmering in the light.

"I don't know if this is what I should be doing. What if a job comes open at—"

"It's not going to, honey, not until the economy turns around. You've been offered a job you can't refuse. Why are you fighting it?"

"Because it's Jaime Dalton, Mom, the one person I actively hate, and now I've sold my soul to him."

"You always did have a wild imagination, Cassandra. Jaime is a good man who obviously needs help. He chose you. Give him some credit at least."

"I don't know if I have any credit left. But I'll give him a month, and if he's the same old Jaime, I'm coming home."

"I guess that's better than hiding in the bathroom until the driver gives up and goes away."

"How did you know I was thinking about doing just that?"

"Because, my daughter, I've known you your

entire life, and Jaime Dalton is the one person who scares the shit out of you. Now grab your gear; the meter's running."

"Love you, Mom."

"I know, love you too, and give Jaime my love. Tell him to kick some Packer ass." Leave it to her mother to see the upside of knowing a professional football player.

Seeing the Packers humiliated each year was what she lived for.

"I'll do that, Mom." Cass whipped the zipper closed on her rolling case and grabbed her carry-on tote and her purse. She hugged her mother and headed out to meet the driver.

The limo in the drive surprised her. She'd expected a car — a regular car — or a taxi, certainly not a limo. Nor did she expect the stir the early morning visit would cause among the neighbors out for their morning walks before heading off to work.

"My daughter is going to work for Jaime

Dalton," her mother shouted to Mrs.

Perkins next door; there was pride in her voice. "She's going to Miami."

"Have fun, Cass. That Jaime Dalton has a cute ass. Tell him I said that, okay?" Mrs. Perkins was somewhere in her seventies, still very active, with a wicked sense of humor and was man crazy.

"I'll do that, Mrs. P."

"Have a good time, dear, and don't do anything I wouldn't do."

"Thelma, don't scare the girl, you know there isn't much out there you wouldn't do."

"Ready, miss?" The driver took her large case and steered her to the back of the car.

His eyes were laughing, though his face betrayed nothing. Cass decided the day just could not get any weirder.

"I guess it's now or never," she told him just before he closed her into the car, where she found herself face-to-face with her mortal enemy. "Hello, Jaime. Mrs. Perkins says to tell you, you have a nice ass, and my mother says to kick some Packer ass." A light flickered behind the deep honey-colored eyes, and with a flick of his wrist, Jaime let the window down and leaned out. "I love you, Mrs. Perkins. When I come back home, I'm taking you out for a night on the town. Mrs. Pendleton, I vow to do my absolute best to grind those Packers into the ground. And I'll take care of your daughter too."

Cass watched as Mrs. Perkins turned a very brilliant shade of red, but the smile on her face was infectious. As for her mother, well, all Cass could do was sink back in the seat and pretend she wasn't related. "Jaime, dear, forgive me, but I don't think you are man enough to take care of my Cass. She's a special kind of difficult."

"Well, I'll give it my best try," he shouted in reassurance.

"You do that, and remember about the Packers. I'm holding you to that."

"Your mother is a hoot. I always liked that

about her." Jaime was still smiling when they exited her street and pulled onto the highway.

"Yes, well, we all have our crosses to bear." Embarrassed to the roots didn't quite cover how Cass was feeling at that moment. "And just in case you forget, I'll remind you that you have a date with Mrs. Perkins next time you're in town. When will that be exactly?"

He just smiled that evasive smile of his. "Have you eaten? I have breakfast. Or coffee. It's too early to talk agendas."

"Jaime…"

"What happened to Mr. Dalton? I think since this is a business arrangement maybe we should stick to a more formal relationship in public."

"Well, we're not in public, we're in the back of a car. I can call you anything I want."

"I've been called a lot of things in the back of a car, but never 'Mr. Dalton.'" The lewd meaning behind his words didn't escape her. "Besides, Miss Pendleton, if we start now, there will be no slip-ups later."

"Lord forbid your people know we have a previous relationship. And since we are on the subject, will I be scheduling your private affairs as well? If so, pull over now and I'll walk home."

"Are you implying we have had a previous relationship? Please, don't flatter yourself. You were just the annoying girl I had to deal with every single day for thirteen years. We had no relationship. As for handling my privates, we'll just have to discuss that later as well."

"You are a pig, Jaime…"

He wagged his finger at her. "Mr. Dalton."

"Fine. You are a pig, Mr. Dalton."

"Why, thank you, Miss Pendleton. Now would you care for a cup of coffee or something to eat before we reach the airport?"

"Do you have any bacon? I'd love some dead pig." She knew it was a stupid retort, but damned if he didn't bring out the child in her.

"Ah, a woman after my own heart." He

opened a stocked buffet. "Help yourself."

* * * * *

Despite her taunt, Cass did little justice to the breakfast he'd picked up. She picked at the biscuit and nibbled on the ham before putting the sandwich down to concentrate on the scenery flashing quickly past. She turned down coffee in favor of orange juice, then asked for tea. He hadn't thought to include a pot of tea.   He quietly studied her for the rest of the trip. Several times, she caught him staring at her and gave him what he remembered as her death stare. Then she began to fidget in her seat, she shifted often, tucking her skirt or tugging at the cardigan she wore over an ivory-colored blouse. After thirty minutes of watching her, he couldn't stand the constant fidgets any longer.

"Are you always this jittery? Or do I make your skin crawl?" She turned those damned blue soul-searing eyes of hers on him as if he really were the devil incarnate. Did she actually dislike him?

"I've never flown before. I'm just nervous and not hungry." The heat in her eyes gave way to uncertainty. "I'm sorry."

"Don't be, I didn't know, I guess I am so used to flying that I never considered … okay, if it's any comfort we'll be on a private jet. We'll drive right up to the plane and sit in leather seats with television and anything else you might need. No going through security lines, no screaming babies. It's usually a three-hour flight, depending on takeoff clearance, of course, and weather. We should be in Miami by noon eastern time and from there a limo to my house, where lunch will be waiting."

"Okay, good, I think. But what about turbulence, and what if…"

"Relax, Cass, I've flown a couple hundred times, nothing is going to happen."

"You promise."

"I promise, and there will be liquor if you

need it. And a bed if that will help." Was it his fault that she heard that wrong? At least she began to relax. *Note to self. Taunting Cass Pendleton distracts her.* Check and double check.

"Miss Pendleton." She fixed him with that evil gleam of hers that he remembered as Cass throwing down the gauntlet.

"What?"

"I'm Miss Pendleton, not Cass or Cassandra, or any of the secret little names you call me."

"I have never had any secret names for you. Just because you had some not-so-nice names for me doesn't mean I stooped to that level."

"No, that's right, I remember now, you preferred calling me names to my face."

"I never…"

"Fatty, fatty, two by four, among others."

"Oh, I did that?" He didn't remember.

"A couple of times, usually when you were with other jocks."

"Oh. Well, for what it's worth. I didn't think

you were fat then. And you certainly aren't fat now."

"Look, Jaime, can we just put that all in the past? Most of my memories of you are painful. If we are going to work together, then we need to bury the hatchet, so to speak."

"You brought it up." Her memories of him were painful? Really? She'd been the aggressor more often than not. She'd been the one who'd tormented him with her need to outdo him at all costs.

"And for that I'm incredibly sorry."

"Well, Miss Pendleton, I guess a fresh start is a good idea. I'm sorry for the things I did in the past, and if you can find it in your heart to forgive me, maybe we can begin our professional relationship on even footing."

"I think I can manage that, Mr. Dalton." And with that, she went back to looking out the window. She didn't offer an apology for the things she'd done in return, but at least she stopped fidgeting.

Chapter Three

Miami wasn't what Cass thought it would be. She'd always imagined a hot and humid tropical paradise with glimmering buildings and fancy cars, but that wasn't the case at all. The weather in late May was very close to the weather at home. With highs reaching into the low eighties, but with a sea breeze, she hardly felt it. The humidity was low, but Jaime assured her that in the middle of summer the days could become almost unbearable, again not much different from home.

The city was beautiful from the air, lots of blue and white framed by turquoise water.

On the ground, though, Miami was like any other city, with fast-food restaurants and discount stores. Again, Jaime informed her that the Miami she saw on television did exist, just not in this particular area.

The drive to his home was stop and go, as city streets turned to suburbia, then to grand estates. The driver proceeded through the estates until the sky and the horizon became one before pulling into a sweeping circular drive, the security gates standing open in welcome.

The house wasn't huge by the neighborhood's standards — white stucco walls with teal Spanish tiles, and a fountain in the courtyard. Sort of low key and highbrow at the same time, with palm trees and an almost ocean view, Cass thought.

"Welcome to my home." Without waiting for the driver, Jaime stepped out of the car and held his hand out to her. In awe of not only the house but also his manner, she took it and slid out into the bright sunlight. "I'll have Alicia put your things in the guest suite, and after lunch we'll get down to business, if that's all right with you?"

"I'll be living here, then?" Somehow she imagined a little apartment nearby sort of arrangement, not an on the premises deal.

"Do you have a problem with that?" Jaime turned to her, real concern on his face.

"Believe me, Cass, this is a big house; I have plenty of room. It'll be almost like you have your own apartment, and the doors lock. Not that there is any danger of midnight visitors."

"I guess it will be fine. I won't have to learn to drive in a strange city; that's a plus ... I guess."

"And you won't have far to commute to work, just down the hallway." He thought that was a plus? The enormity of the situation was starting to overwhelm her. What exactly was he wanting of her? What were the hours? Did he really mean available to him twenty-four seven? Maybe she should have gotten a contract before allowing herself to be hauled halfway across the country to be at her worst enemy's beck and call.

"Ah, Alicia, *mi corazón*." A beautiful dark-skinned woman stood in the door, her smile huge as she hugged Jaime as if he were the conquering hero returned from war. Her eyes sparkled with affection, and after she spotted Cass, her gaze became territorial. His live-in lover? Great. This was going to be fun. "Alicia, this is Miss Pendleton. She's my new personal assistant, and will be living in the guest suite. Cass, this is Alicia, my personal chef and housekeeper. Anything you want, Alicia will be happy to get for you."

"You didn't tell me to expect two for lunch, Jaime." She pronounced his name with an h sound; her hand rested on his upper arm, clearly marking him as hers.

"Didn't I?" Jaime patted her hand and swirled her back into the house. "Oh well, we'll just have to scare Miss Pendleton something up, won't we."

"Yes, Jaime, as you wish." However, her body language said differently as she flounced away into the house.

"Don't mind Alicia; she's very protective of me."

"Oh, is that what you call it? Looked more like

proprietary to me," Cass said as the driver set her bags on the landing. Jaime tipped him, grabbed her larger bag, and guided her inside.

"She's just seen too many women try to take advantage of me, that's all."

"Like I have any urge to do anything with you."

He smiled, his lips stretching into a predatory-type grin; she'd seen that grin before, and if memory served, whatever prompted that grin would not be nice.

"You have nothing to fear on that count, Miss Pendleton. I'd rather play with one of the gators in the canal." He left her standing in the large, open marble foyer, her mouth hanging open.

* * * * *

"But Jaime, you hired me to cook only for you. I won't cook for one of your tramps. And what do you see in her anyway? She is frumpy and bland." Alicia waited until Cass left the kitchen before she lit into him, her accent, usually very light, seeping into her rant. "And she didn't like my *vaca frita*. I don't like people who don't like my food."

"For what it's worth, Cass isn't one of my tramps. Since when have I brought a woman here anyway? I hired her to help me keep my suddenly overflowing life in some sort of order. In her defense, she threw up three times on the plane. Give her time to get over the trip before you have her drawn and quartered."

"She is still frumpy, and her hair is frizzy. I don't like her."

"Jeez, Alicia, don't pull this jealous crap with me, okay? I'm not going down that road with you … again. You are a talented cook, but my life is *my* life. Don't butt in where you aren't needed."

"Do you feel that way, Jaime? I mean, you are choosing that … that … that thing over me." Alicia whipped off her apron and flung it at him.

"Wait a minute, Alicia. What the hell? I'm not choosing anyone, not you or her. I hired you both to work for me, not the other way around."

Somehow, he didn't think that would diffuse the situation. Not that he understood how there was a situation. "You need to be professional and put aside your—"

"I need to be professional? I saw how you looked at her. Like she was ice cream and you were just dying to lick her up. I will not work under these conditions. If you won't get rid of her, then I quit." Alicia thrust her hip toward the cabinet, her arms set firmly in a defensive stance, her chin rigid, and fire in her eyes.

What in the hell was going on here? He hadn't even been in the door thirty minutes, and it was full-scale mutiny. Who was next? The gardener?

"Listen, I have a day full of meetings tomorrow. I've been out of the country for the last month, and I'm tired. You came in on short notice and got the house ready and fixed a great spread. I'm sure you're tired too. Let's just think this thing through."

"No, Jaime, it's the frumpy floozy or me. I

won't work for a man who flaunts his whores under my nose. I mean, we've been together three years. I just won't stand for it. That *puta* is not welcome in my kitchen."

"So that's it, then?" Now he understood; somehow he'd missed the signs. Alicia, always so eager to please him and only him; he should have figured it out sooner. "I'll have Miss Pendleton send your severance check tomorrow. Please leave your keys, and for what it's worth, Alicia, I'm sorry it came to this. I'll give you a reference, of course."

"You prick. You *are* choosing that *puta* over me." He narrowly dodged the sugar bowl as it sailed past his head to shatter against the wall.

"I'm choosing Miss Pendleton over you, yes. And I'm taking that out of your check. Throw something else and I'll have you arrested." He clenched his hands, his voice rumbling in his chest as he growled in frustration. Her eyes turned round, fear replaced fury. Often he wondered what he looked like at times like this; the stance had served him well most of his life, on and off the football field. This was the first time he remembered ever using it on a woman, though.

"I'm sorry, Jaime. I misspoke. I don't want to lose my job. I like it here." Her voice turned pleading, but he saw through her to the petty woman beneath the pretty face and charming accent.

"I'm sorry too, Alicia. I'll walk you out." He took her arm and waited for her to pull his keys off her ring before he helped her into her car. Tears streamed prettily down her face before she drove away. There was nothing he could do about it now.

"Was it something I said?" Cass said from behind the counter, her voice so soft she startled him. He heard the sound of china clinking together, as she cleaned up the broken dish.

"I guess it was a long time coming. I just didn't notice." He turned to the dishes left sitting in the sink and absently started water running. "I don't suppose you can cook? No? Then I guess I have one more job for you, and we should probably have someone out to change the security code at the gate, maybe the locks. I don't know if she has a second set of keys lying around."

"I'm sorry if I caused this." She stood then, carrying the dustpan filled with debris and depositing it in the trash bin near the back door.

"Don't worry about it. Alicia is … well I seem to attract women like her. Beautiful, vain, possessive." He scrubbed the dishes and left them drying on the rack. "Anyway, that's over and we have an appointment downtown in an hour if you want to change or do something with your hair."

"Why do I need to change? What's wrong with my hair?" Dear Lord, did the woman not have a single clue? "Nothing, Miss Pendleton, nothing at all."

Chapter Four

By "appointment," Jaime meant they would be reenacting that scene from *Pretty Woman* in which Julia Roberts is made to feel inferior by tiny, trendy saleswomen in upscale boutiques. The only difference being that she wasn't turned away because Jaime was famous, and his credit card had no limit. However, that didn't mean the ladies — and she used that term very loosely — didn't look at her as if she were something they'd stepped in.

"Everything from the bottom up, shoes, underthings, business attire for Miami and for up north, casual, at least three cocktail dresses, and swimsuits," he ticked off to the small band of women who were completely ignoring her.

"No swimsuits." She shouted over the din of chatter as the women sized her up and started off in different directions.

"This is Miami, Miss Pendleton, water is everywhere. What do you plan to swim in if you have no suit? Of course, there is only one acceptable answer to that question." He wiggled his eyebrows, a knowing smirk on his lips.

"Nothing," she said and immediately wished she hadn't walked headfirst into that trap. "I mean, swimsuits aren't necessary. I don't swim."

"I've seen you swim, Cass." Confusion looked nice on him.

"I didn't say I can't swim, I said I don't swim. I'm allergic to chlorine, severely allergic to chlorine to the point of hospitalization."

"Oh. *Ooh*. Okay, that explains that," he said cryptically. "Cass, the pool at the house is a saltwater pool. I had it converted when I bought the house. It's perfectly safe and much cheaper to maintain too."

"I wouldn't have taken you for someone who cared about low maintenance costs. Especially after this little trip." The shoes the ladies were dragging in were sure to run in the thousands-of-dollars range. "And why do I need all of these clothes, when I'm going to be your little office helper? Where am I going to wear sequins and rhinestones to anyway?"

"Well, after this afternoon, I've decided that I'm promoting you to more than just a personal assistant. I'm promoting you to bodyguard and constant companion as well as my secretary."

"So let me get this straight. I'm to be Pepper Potts to your Tony Stark, then? Are you out of your mind? No, don't answer that."

"Did I mention I was adding another twenty grand a year to your salary?"

"Jaime..." She heard the whine escape her mouth. He was infuriating, argumentative, nauseating, and now somehow he'd added controlling to his lists of faults.

And she let him do it.

"Then it's agreed." His massive chest heaved

as if he'd been holding his breath.

"Miss Pendleton gets the best. I want her to look like the class act she is, and sexy. I can't have my new personal assistant looking anything but ravishing." He snapped his fingers and two of the women swooned on the spot.

"Damn it, Jaime, why are you acting like this?" Frustrated beyond belief, Cass finally snapped. She dug in the heel of her serviceable black pumps and refused to look at any of the clothes that were being shoved in front of her.

"Acting like what? And that's Mr. Dalton to you." He narrowed his eyes to almost a squint, the golden orbs seeming to glow with some inner fire as he fried her to the spot.

His face turned hard, intimidating—almost cruel. But she'd seen it before. He'd worn that very same expression the first time they'd met. He'd just pulled her hair and tried to blame it on her.

"I'm sure that face scares the hell out of your

opponents—but, Jaime Dalton, I am immune. Now stop acting like a controlling dick. I'm not taking on any responsibilities until I see a contract, and I'm not trying on anything that I don't pick out myself. If you want me to work for you, stop treating me like a child or put me on a plane home." She placed her hands on her hips and stared down the one sales girl who gasped and looked at her as if she were committing some sort of criminal offense. "Oh get over it. He's just an ass, not a god."

"Are you quite done with your little hissy fit?"

"That tears it. I'm going home." She took her bag off the sofa in the private fitting area and started for the door, but before she made it two steps, he stopped her with the grin she remembered so well from school. His take-no-prisoners grin that said he held all the cards. Which he did. This time.

"How are you getting there? I thought you were broke." That's what made him a great quarterback. He always found his opponent's weakness and used it against him.

"I'll file kidnapping charges."

"Go ahead—no one will believe you."

"And why is that, do you think?

"For one you're short, pear-shaped with no breasts to speak of, frumpy, and old."

"I'm the exact same age as you." She couldn't dispute the short and pear-shaped part. "And my breasts are real, unlike the silicone bimbos you usually date."

"Cass, be reasonable." He sighed almost as if defeated, but she knew better. He was just changing tactics. Now came the cajoling, wheedling portion of the program, where he pretended to be her best friend and have her best interests at heart.

"And that tactic won't work either. I took debate with you, in case you've forgotten. I know all of your tricks, Jaime. Just play straight with me; that's all you have to do. I don't like being lied to and I don't like being played. You play nice and I'll play nice.

Deal?" She waited while he seemed to think it over. Of course, he could just be plotting a different line of offense; she really couldn't be sure.

"Okay, fine. Cass, you win. If you pick a few things, nice things, I'll butt out. My lawyer is going to meet us this evening to go over the contract I asked him to draw up last night, and if you don't like it, we'll rewrite it or I'll send you home."

"And that bullshit about being your bodyguard against loose women?"

"Well, you are a ball-buster. You'd be great at it." He grinned again, one of his sweet little-boy grins that melted hearts and butter. "Anyway, I'm going to leave my card. Get what you need for a summer in Miami, and I'll pick you up later. All right?"

"All right." Cass waited for the other shoe to

be thrown at her. He left the boutique without another word. Too bad the sales help at the boutique didn't follow his lead.

*****

From the little coffee shop across the street from the boutique, Jaime was able to watch Cass's progress without anyone thinking he was a pervert. The small table by the front window faced the only unobstructed window of the boutique, and the hustle inside was reassuring. The guilt he felt for bullying her was fleeting, as was deserting her to a bunch of she-cats.

Though an obvious fish out of water, Cass could handle herself, and the ladies in the shop would respect his money even if they didn't respect the woman spending it. She would emerge a butterfly from a drab gray pencil-skirt cocoon.

Two hours and three coffees later, Cass did emerge, but not as a butterfly. She was the same drab caterpillar he'd left behind. If the bulging bags she balanced were any indication, though, there was bound to be at least one butterfly packed in there somewhere.

Jaime pulled his cell phone out of his pocket and hit the button for her number, already programmed in the number three spot. He watched as she struggled to find her own, hidden deep in her purse, a smile playing at his lips. She mouthed the word *Fuck* when she saw his name, but she answered anyway.

"I saw that," he smirked into his phone, meaning her lack of grace. "Coffee shop across the street." He hung up, but not before he caught her one-finger salute.

"Your girlfriend?" A passing barista joined him as he watched her cross the street and head his direction.

"Personal assistant, actually, and bound to be a pissed-off one too. Got anything sweet and strong to make up for leaving her to the piranha?"

"Sure, she looks like a caramel-macchiato type to me. And a cranberry scone."

"Sounds good; make it a grande." He handed off a different card just as Cass stumbled into the shop, looking highly agitated and more frazzled than usual.

"If you ever do that to me again, I will kill you. I know many and varied types of poison, and I will be out of the country before the cops even know enough to suspect me," she said, panting from a combination of exertion and frustration. Her lips were pinched, her eyes glowing. Oh yeah, he remembered that look well. He'd seen it directed at himself many, many times.

"Careful, Miss Pendleton. You wouldn't want someone overhearing you threaten Miami's current favorite son. Where will you be when I turn up dead?"

"Prison is preferable to what I just went through, I assure you." She looked up just as the barista set a large mug of steaming caffeine in front of her. "Oh God, that smells wonderful. Thank you."

"I ordered you a scone. You've hardly eaten all day. And I have one more appointment, and then we're off to meet my lawyer for dinner." Jaime signed the credit card slip, leaving a very generous tip.

"Smells nice and I think my stomach might be ready to forgive you for this morning." She sliced into the scone with a plastic spoon and scooped a bite into her mouth, her face a mask of unadulterated pleasure. "Oh, heaven, how did you know I love cranberries?"

"Lucky guess, I guess."

"It was the barista, wasn't it? You aren't that intuitive."

"You can't blame a guy for trying. Let me know when you're ready to move on. I've reserved a couple of hours for you at a day spa. I have to go into the front office and sign some papers. I'll pick you up at six, I'd like you to be wearing something dressy casual for dinner."

"Aye, aye, Cap'n. How much skin should I

show? Oh wait, I have no cleavage to speak of, so that's out of the question. Any way you'd like me to have my hair styled? I assume there is hair and a facial involved in all of this?"

"Leave it long, you look much nicer with long hair than that pixie cut you wore in school, but try to have the frizz tamed down, and Cass, please behave."

"Who? Me?"

"Why do I feel like I'm going to regret the next few months?"

"Probably because you are going to regret the next few months. Unless you stop trying to control me."

"Then stop being a train wreck. And finish your coffee."

Chapter Five

Honestly, two hours of pampering was something Cass decided she could get used to. Though having her hair decision taken out of her hands completely still left her a bit miffed.

Shontal, her hair stylist, had clucked his lips at first, but after clearing away the split ends, he'd changed his tune. The humidity would be a problem for her, but he loaded her down with hair balms and sprays he guaranteed to keep her new and improved hair looking great during a hurricane.

Face and nails were next, then a massage. About halfway through the process she started looking around for Stacey London and Clinton Kelly, feeling as if she'd suddenly turned up on a sneak attack episode of *What Not to Wear*. When it was all over, she was disappointed. Not only because Stacey and Clinton had not jumped out yelling surprise, but because Jaime was waiting for her.

"Well?" she said after waiting for him to comment on the cornflower blue halter dress and the casual upsweep Shontal had hastily arranged after her massage. "Do I meet your standards, Mr. Stark? Or is it back to the drawing board?"

"Well, Pepper, I guess it will have to do. Come on, we're late."

"A 'you look great' or some facsimile thereof would be nice. After all, I played nice and let people rip hair out of places I didn't even know had hair."

"Wow, Cass, you look spectacular. Really, I mean it." He stopped dead and rolled his eyes. Sarcasm was his strong point after all, so why should it bother her so much?

"But for the record, where exactly did they rip hair out of?" She balled up her fist and punched his upper arm, regretting it instantly. "Ouch, Christ, that hurt."

"Yeah, I guess you shouldn't have done that." He held up his arm and flexed it; the muscles beneath rippled into an even harder mass.

"You know, Jaime, I guess you have changed after all. You're an even bigger jerk than I remember."

"I'm Ironman, honey. I get to be a jerk if I want to."

"Oh fuck you."

"Only if you are very lucky or I am very drunk." Jaime opened the door to his sports car for her. "And I mean very, very drunk."

"Asshole…" she shouted, but he closed the door in her face. When he eased into the seat next to her, he was chuckling that evil laugh of his that set her nerves on end. "Will this night ever end?"

"Why? Do you have a date or something? Seriously, Pepper, I can drop you somewhere if you want. Just tell me."

"Just drive. And stop calling me Pepper. You're not Ironman, and I'm not your Girl Friday."

"But that's exactly what you signed up for, to be my Girl Friday and every other day of the week. And while we're at it, let's revisit that idea of you taking on the responsibility of keeping all the crazy women at bay this summer so I can actually get some work done."

"Jaime, seriously, I don't know what you have in mind, but that plot never seems to work in the movies, why do you think it would work in real life?"

"You saw Alicia this afternoon. She thought that because she'd worked for me for the three years I've been here, that we had some sort of relationship. And she's not the first. I mean, don't get me wrong. I love the attention, but after a while it just gets old, know what I mean?"

"Sorry, no. I have no experience with money-hungry women throwing themselves at me, fake boobs first. I guess I can see why a classy guy like you would have a problem with it. I'm told steroids do a number on the package, and the sex drive. I guess you wouldn't want anyone getting the idea that Jaime Dalton isn't exactly the Ironman he thinks he is."

"I don't dope. I work hard for this body. Do you really think I'd risk my career on steroids?" He turned to face her, anger in his eyes. Fun-and-games time had come to an abrupt end.

"How would I know, Jaime? It's not like we've ever been friends. I don't know you all that well, and I don't follow sports."

"Well, I don't. End of discussion."

"Fine," she said, leaning back in her seat and watching as the sun set the city ablaze before it finally sank in the distance. Jaime drove deeper into the city, the silence between them deafening.

"Welcome to South Beach," he said after a while, his voice carrying a hint of pride.

"The Miami you see on television in all its

glory." Art Deco buildings in shades of pink and purple flew past as he drove. People dressed in pastels walked the streets bathed in neon and the last pink rays of the setting sun. For a moment, Cass couldn't catch her breath. Everywhere she looked was a treat for the senses.

"Gorgeous," she breathed, catching sight of the blue water turning rapidly obsidian in the waning light. "Absolutely gorgeous."

"I thought you'd like it here. Everybody likes South Beach. Mitch is meeting us for drinks and dinner in about an hour if you'd like to park and walk out on the sand?"

"I'd love to. I've never seen the ocean before. Did you know that?"

"No, Cass, I didn't."

Somehow, she didn't like the way he looked at her in that instant, almost as if he pitied her. She didn't like how his voice became soft, almost seductive, like a caress.

"I'm glad I get to be the one who took your

beach virginity." And just like that, Jaime Dalton reverted to his true form—rotten to the core.

* * * * *

Her legs were shapely, lightly muscled, and honey golden. She tugged her skirt up her thighs and danced into the calm surf, her laughter infectious. He wanted to join her, but he didn't have the luxury of being able to pull his jeans up. If Mitch weren't waiting, he wouldn't let a little thing like soaked clothes get in the way.

The light breeze teased her hair, pulling strands from the neat twist that framed her face setting off her smile. Had he ever actually seen Cass Pendleton smile? he wondered fleetingly. His heart quickened a beat or two when she hiked her skirt up too high, revealing blue lace, cheek-hugging panties.

Oh, for God's sake, this was Cassandra-fucking-Pendleton, who was too short, too curvy, and way too mouthy for his taste. But she had a nice ass.

He stifled a groan, reminding himself he wanted Cass because she was the woman least likely to try and get in his bed, and here he was thinking about her ass and wondering if that cleavage she claimed not to have was actually hers or some miracle bra giving her a boost.

"Hey, Pepper, we have to go," he shouted over the sound of the water and the wind and her laughter. "Mitch already ordered drinks."

"What happened to meeting in an hour?" She trudged into the sand and scooped up her discarded sandals and slipped them on, oblivious to the sand clinging to her legs.

"He's early." He shrugged, Mitch Abrams had a tendency to run early, that's why Jaime liked doing business with him. "I'm starving. Let's go eat."

"Sure." Her face twisted into a pained expression.

"What's wrong?"

"The sand is itchy, and I can't get it off."

"Just wait until we get to the sidewalk, trying to get it all off while standing in it is futile."

Once they reached the sidewalk, she began swiping at the fine grains but with little success. "Oh for fuck's sake. Here, give me a leg." The look she gave him told him she'd rather be fed to the gators, but she kicked off her sandal and offered her leg to him. Jaime bent on his knee and starting sweeping sand from her knee down. He hadn't expected her skin to be so soft or smooth that he would want to explore higher. "Mmm, there ya go. Best I can do. The rest will fall off after it's dry. At least it better, because I don't want any of it in my car."

"How magnanimous of you, my lord and master."

"I like the sound of that. I give you permission to call me either 'Lord' or 'Master.' Master Ironman has a great ring to it."

"Did anyone ever tell you that your ego is so huge you suck all the life out of them?"

"You. All day long. And frankly, Pepper, it's getting old."

"Stop calling me Pepper."

"When you start calling me Lord Ironman." He took her arm, tucked it into the crook of his elbow, and led her down the street. She was steaming and didn't seem to notice his touch.

"You really are an asshole, and here I thought I was being unkind in my assessment of your character, but no … I was right." She shook her arm free and walked into the restaurant without another word to him.

Jaime suppressed the urge to throttle her. Though he was sure he'd be acquitted of her death, due to the fact that she was as annoying as shit. However, he was pretty sure his career wouldn't survive the scandal, so he tucked his hands into his pockets until the urge passed.

The hostess smiled at him; her pretty blue eyes licking him all over restored his faith in womankind. "Hey there, sweetheart, I have a reservation."

"I know, Mr. Dalton. Mr. Abrams is waiting; follow me."

"Anywhere, sweetheart. Just lead the way."

He laughed when Cass mouthed the word *pathetic* before she followed the hostess into the restaurant and thankfully proceeded to ignore him as much as possible the rest of the evening.

Chapter Six

Apparently, "crack of dawn" meant more like somewhere around noon for Jaime. At least that's when Cass finally heard him calling her name from somewhere in the massive house. She lay in her bed, staring up at the blue ceiling while she tried to figure out where her limbs were. She sure as hell didn't feel them, or anything else for that matter, and her mouth tasted like she'd eaten a dirty sock.

Three dirty martinis and a glass of wine with dinner. She remembered that much at least. She also remembered that Jaime drank nothing but water or iced tea all night long while he ordered her drink after drink.

"Prick," she croaked to the ceiling. "Oh God, what time is it?" The clock on the bedside table read a little after eleven. "Pepper! Are you dead in there? If you aren't downstairs in three minutes, I'm coming in."

"Jesus Christ, stop screaming at me," she shouted back and winced as pain shot through her head. "I'm up. I'm up."

"Good. I thought I was going to have to shove you in the shower or something." His voice was very close by. She rolled toward the sound and was startled to see him standing beside her bed, looking sweaty and way too awake after a night of carousing. And just as quickly, she realized she wasn't wearing anything but a pair of blue panties under the sheet that covered her.

"Do I need to ask if you had anything to do with what I'm not wearing?" She wouldn't freak out. She would remain calm, cool, collected. Oh shit, she didn't remember a damn thing about falling into bed.

"Sorry to disappoint you, Pepper, but I left you standing at the door. What you did after you closed it — in my face, I might add — is all on you." He reached for the cover, but she grabbed it and pulled it tight around her body. "But I'm flattered that you include me in your fantasies."

"Why has no one murdered you by now? Or at least taken a soap-filled sock to you?" That was a fun thought. Jaime on the floor, all tied-up and being flogged. "No, on second thought, murder is better. It's more permanent."

"My, but aren't you bloodthirsty in the morning." He leaned against the post at the foot of the bed, his eyes traveling her body, belying his stated disinterest. "Do you always sleep naked? Or just when you're drunk?"

"You got me drunk, you prick, while you were drinking water. You poured enough gin into me to fill a damn bathtub."

"You could have said no at any time."

"That's what your mother should have said the night you were conceived."

"Forget bloodthirsty, you're just plain mean

when you're hungover." The smile left his eyes at her remark. She knew she'd gone too far the second the words left her mouth.

"Get up, Cass. My agent is coming at one, and since you'll be working with him, I want you dressed for business and on your best behavior."

"Yes, Lord Ironman." She remembered that much at least.

"Brownie points for that."

"Goody, I like brownies. Hey, Jaime, I didn't mean that about your mom, and I liked your dad, he was a nice man." Sense was finally returning, and despite her personal feelings for their son, there was no reason to insult his parents.

"Thanks for that. He *was* a good man." He turned to leave, but something else occurred to her.

"Hey, Jaime?"

"Yeah, Pepper?"

"I can't feel my legs. I think I might be paralyzed."

"You are going to be a handful, aren't you?" He grabbed her hand and hauled her up and out of bed so fast she barely had time to drag the sheet with her, much less stay covered.

"There, you're up. Do you think you can manage a shower on your own now, or do you need me to toss you in there after all?"

Her legs were wobbly, but with the help of the bedpost, she managed to stay up.

Unfortunately, that set the gin in her stomach to churning, and she barely made it to the bathroom before it all came back up.

"Note to self: don't give Pepper liquor." She felt warm hands on her shoulders just before he dragged her hair out of the line of fire. "I'm sorry for getting you drunk."

"I think I'll live." Too drained to hold her head up after the last bout, Cass lay against his thigh and waited for the world to stop spinning. After a while, she became aware of his hand gently caressing her back. To her horror, she noticed the sheet lying on the bedroom floor ten feet away. But she didn't have enough energy to care that she was wearing nothing but a pair of blue lace panties while she puked in front of Jaime Dalton.

"I'll call Sam and postpone that meeting." He eased out from under her and headed for the door. "Come down when you're ready. And Cass, I really am sorry."

"I know," she said, but he'd already gone. She wrapped her arms around her breasts and sat on the floor, trying not to think about the tingling sensation his hand caused. Or that despite being hungover and pukey, parts of her body had suddenly decided Jaime Dalton wasn't such a bad person after all. Then she grabbed her own hair and forgot about Jaime Dalton altogether.

* * * * *

Dear God, who would have thought that Cass Pendleton, dressed in nothing but a pair of cheeky panties, would have that kind of effect on him?

Her skin was so soft, her body sleek and trim, with no tan lines that he could see. Either Cass was naturally a golden honey color, or she tanned in the nude. He stifled a groan when the image of her small but incredibly well-formed breasts taunted him.

He did not want Cassandra Pendleton!

Emphatically, without a doubt the last thing on his mind was getting inside Cass Pendleton's panties. His dick had somehow missed that memo. He knew the moment she lost the sheet he was a dead man. Following her into the bathroom had been his first mistake; his second was touching her and letting her touch him.

His thigh tingled where she'd rested her head, and he couldn't even think about the sensation in his calf when her nipple had grazed him. Oh Lord, he couldn't think about this. He couldn't stay in the house knowing she was naked, helpless, and not nearly as mean as she used to be.

He stepped out into the spring air, and

disregarding the storm clouds brewing on the horizon, he dove into the pool still dressed in his workout clothes. The water wasn't frigid like it would be back home. But it wasn't warm either, and through the shock of cold coupled with trying to break the Olympic record for number of laps, Jaime finally found some relief from his own stupidity.

Maybe it wasn't too late. Maybe putting Cass on a plane back home would be for the best. She was clearly miserable here. And she hated him. He'd call Mitch up and have him void the contract, give her three months' severance pay, and send her home. That would be the guilt-free way to go, a win-win scenario for them both.

On his fifteenth lap, he somehow talked himself out of that. Last night had been fun.

More fun than he'd had in a long time. At dinner, she'd ordered a huge steak and a salad and devoured every last bite. He couldn't remember the last time he'd shared a meal with a woman when he didn't feel like the poster boy for one or all of the seven deadly sins.

After Mitch had left, he'd somehow convinced her to dance with him. Of course, that was after the wine, and two martinis. Cass could move with a grace he'd never imagined.

Somehow, he remembered her always dressed in tutus and ballet shoes as a kid. Their paths crossed at McDonalds on the way home from after school activities on many occasions. Maybe that was why she seemed weightless against him.

Maybe she was just drunk and without her usual inhibitions, and he'd taken advantage of that. Goading her to be someone she wasn't by pouring alcohol into her.

Finally, he knew she'd had enough when she fell against him, her body slick with sweat.

Her eyes were alive with a sexuality that, frankly, scared him. She would sleep with him; he knew that even before they left the club. Lord help them both if he took her up on her offer. He brought her home and left her standing in her room. He was proud of himself for his self-control. But this was Cass, not some groupie; if he'd stooped that low, well—he hadn't stooped so low as to seduce Cass; his conscience was clear on that point at least. Of that he could be proud.

Right up until this morning when she didn't come down for breakfast, and still wasn't down after his run. He began to get scared. What if she'd hurt herself? Somehow, fallen out of the window, or drowned in the tub? Or alcohol poisoning? Had she had enough to drink to poison her system? How much alcohol did that even take?

He stood outside her door and started pounding on it, calling her name, making threats for nearly five whole minutes, before she shouted back. He'd been so relieved that he'd opened the door just to make sure. Thinking back, that had been his first mistake of the day, walking into her room while she laid supine, half covered by a sheet, which did little to conceal her curves.

Damn! Jaime plunged back into the water for one last lap. *Stop thinking about her, stop it, fool. Cass Pendleton is evil. She is the most hateful woman in the world. And ugly.*

Damn but she is hideous. She isn't blonde or tall or model thin. And Meathead, she is smarter than you are. How about them apples?

Jaime climbed out of the pool, his inner voice apparently satisfied, his body purged of indecent thoughts of Miss Pendleton. Unfortunately, his stomach took up where his conscience left off.

"Shit," he swore out loud. He'd somehow managed to forget that he'd fired his cook yesterday. No wonder Alicia wasn't in the kitchen singing some catchy Cuban song.

Double damn, he was supposed to send her out a check today or at least get Cass to send her one. On top of that, he'd forgotten to call his agent, Sam, to postpone their meeting until this evening. Now it was probably too late.

He stripped out of his wet clothes and padded

to the back door naked and dripping.

Inside, he checked the clock—after twelve already—Sam would already be halfway here from the airport. He picked up the towel he'd left on the back of a kitchen chair, wrapped it around his nudity, and flung open the refrigerator to see if there was anything he could handle with his limited cooking skills.

There were bottles and bags of things he couldn't identify, but the flank steak wrapped in butcher paper he could handle. Enough vegetables to make a salad filled the drawers, and with any luck, he would find potatoes in the pantry; if not, then he would just have to wing it. After three years, he was finally going to fire up the grill outside and burn something.

Maybe not having a cook was a good thing.

* * * * *

"Not having a cook sucks," Jamie told her the second she stepped into the kitchen. "Why did I fire Alicia?"

"I believe it was because she threw a sugar bowl at your head." Cass sniffed the air, something smelled delicious, and she was amazed that after emptying her stomach, she could even stand the aroma of food. But after standing under the steam jets in the guest shower for nearly an hour, she felt great. "I'm starving. What's to eat?"

"Don't give me that look." Jaime pointed the chopping knife he was using to mutilate tomatoes at her for emphasis. "That look. That one you're giving me now, the one where you think I'm an idiot."

"I have never thought you were an idiot, Jaime, just a jerk; there's a big difference." She stepped around the island and took the knife from him. "Here, those poor tomatoes are dying horrible deaths; let me take over."

"What happened to Lord Ironman?"

"I have no idea what you mean." She took a fresh tomato and sliced the stem end off.

She vaguely remembered calling him

something along those lines, just before she puked her guts up, but he didn't need to know that. "What am I making?"

"Salad. I have steaks on the grill and potatoes in the oven. There's a loaf of some kind of bread in the pantry, I thought we could slather butter on it or something. It's all I know how to cook."

"So either we muddle through, or I should hire a new cook?"

"Something like that. And after Sam leaves, I need to get Alicia a check sent out. I'm thinking three months' salary ought to make her happy."

"She'll probably sell all of your secrets to the tabloids anyway."

"She doesn't know any of my secrets. She didn't live here, and I didn't bring people over. She just came in, cleaned the house, and prepared a meal or two every day."

"Oh, she knows something, I'm sure. She most likely went through all of your stuff while you were out. She read your mail at the very least."

"How do you know that?"

"Because that's what I would have done; that's what everyone does when they're left alone in someone else's house. Go through their stuff. Alicia knows where you've buried at least one body, you can bet the farm on that."

"What the fuck are you talking about? Are you still drunk?"

"Oh come on, Jaime, you are not a Pollyanna. People are people. Of course, she knows something about you that you would rather your fans didn't find out about. That you're gay and in love with a country music star maybe, or worse, that you're secretly married to three different women, none of whom know the others exist, that you cheated on your taxes last year, or that you pick your nose and eat the boogers."

"I did not cheat on my taxes."

"Well, that's a relief. I was worried that you might be hiding something terrible."

"Pepper, you talk too much. Has anyone ever

told you that?"

"It's why I went into teaching in the first place. I like the sound of my own voice.

Well that, and I am addicted to the smell of chalk and white-board markers. The combination is nirvana."

"I'm glad you cleared that up. When the cops ask why, I'll be sure to tell them it was self-defense due to you being a chalk junkie."

"Don't forget those markers. They are the meth of the teaching profession." Thunder rumbled outside, matching the noise in her stomach. Jaime cussed under his breath and ran out to pull the grill under shelter just before the heavens opened up.

The air coming in from the screened-in patio was damp, sweet, and cool. Raindrops fell fat and heavy into the pool; palm fronds swayed in the wind just past the patio.

Contentment washed over her, through her, nearly overwhelming her with its punch.

"No, no, this is not right." The knife in her hand felt suddenly heavy, the walls began to close in. "This is only temporary. Jaime Dalton is still a jerk and is just waiting to pull your hair again, you stupid, silly woman. Tomorrow he'll fire you, and that will be the end of that."

The stern talking to did little to stop the surge of … of, whatever that feeling was, when she watched him battle the flames and the elements. Jaime Dalton could pose for the Ironman poster after all.

Her thoughts were interrupted by a buzzing coming from somewhere in the front of the house. It continued, becoming more insistent.

"Jaime!" she shouted from the doorway, "I think there is some sort of alarm going off. Jaime do you hear me?"

"What kind of alarm? Oh shit, it's the front gate, Sam is here." He raced past her and into the foyer where he spoke into a monitor on the wall near the door. A few moments later, a man dressed in khaki shorts and a rain jacket tumbled in through the front door.

"Sorry about the weather, Sam, but as they say in Miami, wait a minute and it'll change."

Sam wasn't what she pictured. Of course, her only image of an intrepid sports agent was, unfortunately, Tom Cruise. Sam Copeland was, by far, no Tom Cruise.

He was more of a Tom Hanks, though, with wavy dark hair, laughing eyes, and a bit of a paunch and crow's feet. His handshake was strong when Jaime introduced her. His eyes took in every detail before he smiled.

"So this is the new assistant. No offense, Miss Pendleton, but knowing Jaime as well as I do, I expected a tall leggy blonde. Not a petite — what did you say she did? — oh yeah, kindergarten teacher."

"Third grade, Mr. Copeland. I taught third grade." She narrowed her eyes, aware that her hackles were raised. Beyond the fact that he didn't listen very well, something about him was not quite right. Probably his too easy smile that said more used-car salesman than trusted businessman. "Third grade is a tricky year—multiplication, division, and cursive writing come into play."

"Yes, but what do you know about the sports world? Cursive writing isn't half as tricky as negotiating multimillion-dollar endorsement deals and wrangling prima donna athletes."

"Well, Mr. Copeland, if more of your sports heroes would learn cursive writing in the first place, or any writing for that matter, then your job might not be so tricky."

"Pepper! Down, girl. Let Sam enjoy his lunch, and then we'll all sit down and work out how the two of you are going to work together to make my life easier." Jaime stepped beside her and wrapped his arm around her shoulder, easing her back into the kitchen.

"Come on out to the patio, Sam, we'll talk

man things while the woman does the kitchen stuff."

When Sam was safely on the patio, Cass found a soft spot on the underside of Jaime's arm, and with a pinch and a twist, she walked away satisfied with his yelp of pain.

Chapter Seven

Over the course of the next few weeks, Cass fell into a routine that she grew to enjoy. Up in the morning early, to sync up with Sam and work Jaime's publicity and endorsement schedule in with his day-job schedule.

As the summer slowly slid toward July and the imminent start of football season, he was gone more and more, leaving her alone with not as much to do as he had thought. He made good on the promise of a car. A nice, sensible Mercedes wagon. And she found the shopping area closest to the house for groceries and such. Then she found the bookstore, and her world suddenly became right again. There was so much to do that didn't fit into Jaime's job description to keep her busy. Such as learning to cook and filling the empty rooms in Jaime's house with furniture.

On her third day with Jaime, she'd given herself a tour of the house and discovered that in the three years he'd been in the house, he had only bought furniture for a handful of rooms—a den, an office, his bedroom, the guest room she occupied, and a weight room. The house had four more bedrooms, a dining and living room, and a huge room that had no apparent purpose.

At Jaime's suggestion, she started picking out furniture and paint samples. When the food in the fridge had run low and no candidate for a replacement cook had shown up, she decided she could figure that out too.

The bookstore gave her access to everything she needed to wear the different hats inside Jaime Dalton's empire.

Jaime himself posed less of a problem as the days went by. At first, he was constantly underfoot and tormenting her. Somehow, she'd managed to make it through the first week without killing him. Then that glorious day came when she put him on a plane to Los Angeles to film a commercial. His workout schedule accelerated, as June began to wind into July, and he was gone most of the days he wasn't posing for posters or volunteering with the charities he supported.

His life was busy and complicated. After two weeks of living with him, she finally understood why he needed someone to help him keep track of his appointments. Sam was just the person who got him extra work. He didn't call to wake him up, after a late night with members of his team or the one or two bimbos he went out with, to make it to his appointments. Or to meet with the president of the United States to receive an award for his work with the Boys and Girls Club.

However, just because Jaime's life was complicated, that didn't mean hers was. After synchronizing schedules with Sam and texting the daily doings to Jaime's phone, she actually had very little to do.

In short, Cass was bored. Even verbal warfare with Jaime had lost its appeal, after she figured out he was still just a restless kid who needed something to do to keep him out of her hair. Then came that day, while sitting at a red light, the back of her soccer mom car filled with paint supplies and groceries, that she realized her soccer kid was Jaime Dalton.

That day in mid-June, she came to another realization that bothered her even more than the fact that she'd somehow become Jaime's mother. Jaime was avoiding her. The big bad scary football player was avoiding little old her, and she had no idea why.

Well, besides her need to argue with him every time he opened his mouth. Or her almost obsessive need for his approval of each room as she brought it to life. After a month of having no one else to talk to about the things that bothered her, she included him in her observations on the daytime television schedule and her sudden fascination with the strange goings on on *The Jersey Shore*. Somehow, she identified a little too closely with Sookie, or Snookie, or whatever the hell her name was. Except for the slutty clothes, big hair, and the orange skin, of course.

Now that she thought about it, all of those clothes she'd bought her first day in Miami were still hanging in her closet, unworn. She'd found clothes at the local Target that fit her stay-at-home-mom life much better than the sexy secretary stuff she'd found in the boutique. One day she was going to haul out the black cocktail dress and wear it to vacuum the new carpet in the living room.

She'd even found time to use the pool, and suits that didn't show as much skin as those at the boutique. It really was nice to take a swim without having third-degree chemical burns everywhere her clothes touched her.

Of course, her mother had started letting her

calls go to voicemail, as had two of her college friends who had real lives.

Yes, Cass decided, she was bored out of her ever-loving mind and was ready to stake Jaime Dalton to a palm tree outside and watch him burst into flame. Oh wait, that would be one of the vampires on that dirty HBO show.

Cass banged her head on the steering wheel after this realization and drove herself home, where she unloaded the trunk. And like a good little SAHM, she went inside to whip up a good meal for her man in thirty minutes or less. Rachel Ray would be so proud.

* * * * *

For nearly four weeks, Jaime had been avoiding his new personal assistant like the plague she was. For four weeks, he made sure he was out of the house before she came down to occupy his office. He came home for lunch, usually to find her on her hands and knees digging in the flowerbeds, or the kitchen cabinets.

Lately, she was up to her elbows in paint, and if he saw one more fabric sample, he might have to throttle her. She talked a lot. About everything, from what books she found at Barnes and Noble to the dating woes of the guy who mixed her paint at The Home Depot. He now knew the Cassandra rankings of all of the coffee shops nearby, and just how far it was on foot to the library. Hell, he didn't even know where the library was located.

Somehow, she managed to find the art community and was slowly sneaking in paintings and objects that looked suspiciously like naked sticks. One day soon, he was terribly afraid that he was going to come home and find she'd taken up dog walking for the neighbors.

Cass was bored.

She didn't say anything to that effect, but he could tell. Her brain was moving too fast. And if he hadn't known before he decided it would be a good idea to hire her, he knew now that when Cassandra was bored, she drove everyone around her crazy.

Unfortunately, for the last four weeks, everybody was just him.

It was his fault. He'd taken her away from her family, her friends, and any possible mind-numbing but Cass-fulfilling job she might have found at home to handle what, to him, was a major problem, but to her was a very tiny portion of her day.

So out of guilt and to get her to leave him alone, he gave her his credit card and turned her loose on the empty rooms in his house. Apparently, painting, cooking, and gardening weren't enough to occupy her mind. So, she waited for him to come home, exhausted from endorsement shootings, his morning workout, his afternoon workout, and the one or two dates he'd somehow managed to sneak off to, to talk to him. About everything.

And exactly why he felt guilty for sneaking out to see other women, or just to get away from her, began to fester within his already overwrought personality. Soon he would snap and do something very, very bad to Cass Pendleton. Something that would involve the city dredging the canal behind the house and him fleeing the country.

Finally, the first day of July, about two weeks before he had to report for training camp, he walked into his house and realized he didn't recognize it anymore. He found her in the garage, stripping varnish off a perfectly good dresser and talking to the television that was on in the laundry room. He didn't even want to know when or why she put a television in the laundry room, but there it was, and Cass was telling a judge on one of the daytime shows exactly what she thought of his ruling in very purple language.

"Okay, enough is enough," he said over the chatter, but she didn't seem to hear.

"Pepper, turn that damned thing off, or I'll … I'll throw it in the pool."

"Who licked the red off your lollipop?" she retorted, but she turned the set off. "There, are you happy now?"

"Immensely. Now as I was saying, enough is enough. I can't take the odor of paint or the sound of sanding or the constant television garbage another minute—"

"Is that why you've been messing around with my stuff? Because you hate the smell?" It was a strange question that caught him off guard.

"Uh, no. What the hell are you talking about?"

"I keep finding paint cans and varnish open, or not where I left them. Once a whole can was spilt on the vanity I'd just finished sanding." She pointed the TV remote at him in an accusatory fashion, her eyes narrowed in a Cass-going-for-his-jugular sort of way.

"And that's what I'm talking about—this is borderline obsessive behavior, and it's driving me nuts. Go upstairs, wash the stink off, and put on something that doesn't scream bag lady. You have thirty minutes; after that I'm throwing you in the shower and dressing you."

"Who's going to make me?" She laughed at him — seriously — laughed right in his face and went back to scraping the dresser as if he hadn't said a thing.

"Okay then, just remember that you asked for this," Jaime bellowed just before he lifted her in the air and flung her over his shoulder. She kicked him in the private parts and tried to bite him as she struggled and cursed, but a slap to her ass settled her down for the long trip up two sets of stairs to her room. He deposited her on the bed without a second of guilt, even when he saw murder and other types of mayhem in her eyes.

"Thirty minutes, Pepper. Don't make me come and get you. Because you will not like what I'll do to you."

"Prick." She threw her shoe at him.

"So you keep telling me." He dodged the second on the way out the door. "Thirty minutes."

He paced the foyer watching the stairs for thirty minutes, looking at his watch so often he thought he would wear it out. When the minute hand swept around to the half mark, he started to climb the stairs.

Cass, dressed in a pair of white Capri pants and a deep blue peasant-style top with matching sandals and a turquoise bag, met him on the first landing. Curiosity filled her eyes when she swept over him, noticing his khaki pants and button-down team shirt.

"You know all you had to do was tell me we had an appointment somewhere." She passed him on the landing, her hair swinging in a loose braid between her bared shoulder blades.

"I should have, I'm sorry. It's just that watching you putter around the house is driving me crazy, and the constant noise from the television isn't helping." There he'd said it. She was driving him crazy. "I brought you down here and left you at loose ends most of the day. I'm sorry for that too. I guess I thought the job would be bigger than it is."

"For you, I'm sure it is. You're the one living this schedule. And if what you keep telling me is true, then it's only going to get worse for you. I got that much. But between you and Sam, all I have to do is keep your schedule updated and send you reminder texts." She shrugged, looking up at him from the foyer. "I'll figure something out."

"And that is why we're going out. I have a surprise for you. Come on." He took her arm and led her out to his car, where he held the door for her. Mentally patting himself on the back for solving both of their problems at once. Of course, if he had a brain in his head, he'd have thought of this weeks ago. But as Cass was fond of reminding him, he didn't have two brain cells rubbing together, especially when it came to her.

"I'm well aware of your surprises, Jaime. Tell me where we're going."

"No, you'll just have to wait and see. It's not far, Cass, just sit on your hands for a little while, and if you don't like it, then you can strangle me — but at least give it a chance."

"This doesn't involve gators, does it?"

"Well, there will be things with teeth, but not of the reptilian variety."

"Fine, just drive. I have to finish that dresser, and I'm planning to make chicken for dinner. And there's a *Real Housewives* marathon coming on tonight that I want to watch."

"Yeah? Which one, Orange County or Atlanta?"

"Atlanta, of course." She looked at him funny as she buckled her seat belt, but was quiet the rest of the way.

When he pulled into the parking lot at the old school that housed the area Boys and Girls Club of America, he could feel her curiosity bubbling, almost as if it were a living creature. "Is this the club you volunteer with?"

"Yeah, I go outside and toss the ball around to the kids and tell them to stay in school and work hard. But, Cass, I think you can do more here than even I can."

"How so?" She watched a group of little kids walk in single file from one building to another, a wistful look on her face.

"They need volunteers for the summer, and then when school starts in August, tutors for the afterschool program. I think you might be more than qualified to help out. What do you think?"

"I think I love you, is what I think." Before he could brace himself for impact, she launched herself into his arms. Her lips were so soft when she kissed him, that he almost forgot that she was off limits. "Where do I sign up?" Two hours later, a thoroughly exhausted but incredibly happy woman fell into the seat next to him. "You can thank me anytime. But for right now, how about we go out for dinner. I feel the need to eat something that didn't start life in a can for a change."

"And just like that, the old Jaime opens his mouth and all of his good deeds are undone."

"So that's a no to dinner on the town?"

"God, no, I'm so sick of my cooking I could puke." She laughed, and for the first time in weeks, Jaime felt as if everything in his life was finally falling in place, but knowing Cass, that feeling would only last so long before he started contemplating mayhem once again. For now, he was happy just to have an evening off and a pretty woman to share it with. Even if that woman was Cassandra Pendleton.

"You know, I've been thinking," she said as he pulled out of the parking lot onto the highway.

"That lasted a long time," Jaime replied with a sigh. The look she gave him told him the interruption wasn't appreciated. "I'm sorry; you were saying?"

"I was saying that I think it's time for me to move out of your guest room. I found a nice apartment not far away. I can easily commute in every morning and update your itinerary, check on the house, even do the cleaning and the shopping. You need your space, and I need to get to know the community. Besides, I have all that money you're paying me with nothing to spend it on." She sped through her appeal, looking nervously at him every second or so as if he were somehow actually in control of anything concerning her.

"Well, Cass, you're not a prisoner in my house. If you'd prefer someplace of your own, I can certainly understand. I just thought that the guest room would be convenient is all."

"And you wouldn't have to listen to me talk all the time or the television. And if you wanted to bring a ... a friend home, I won't be underfoot, and vice versa." She looked so happy at the prospect of getting away from him. Every last word of her argument was valid. She had a point. But damned if he wanted to think about that last point. The very idea of Pepper bringing male friends over somehow left a bad taste in his mouth.

"Sounds like a plan. Remind me tomorrow and we'll get the ball rolling. Now what do you have in mind for dinner? I'd like a great big steak and maybe some fried shrimp."

"I don't know. I was sort of thinking Italian."

Cassandra Pendleton always, always had to have the last word, Jaime realized with a sigh. Which was why they stayed far apart. He hated not having the last word.

"I think I know of a place where we can both get what we want."

"Either way, I'm good."

"Pepper, you're killing me. Killing me."

"Just shut up and drive. And for the millionth time, stop calling me Pepper."

Chapter Eight

"I think your moving-out idea is for the best all around." He'd stood in the foyer watching her walk up the stairs after dinner and a movie out. He waited until she reached the landing to add, "Just as soon as you've hired a new cook and a housekeeper, I'll help you find a place, and I'll even spring for the furniture."

That was three nights ago, and Cass hadn't spoken to him since. Asshat. He knew what he was saying. He knew the trouble she'd had finding someone to come here and cook large meals for one person with such a strange schedule. Plus, he hadn't made it easy, with too many restrictions on the hiring process. No males, or recent graduates of any culinary school, or former fast-food workers, and for fuck's sake—his words not hers—no Goddamned vegetarians.

After a couple of weeks of trying to keep Jaime Dalton fed, she now understood some of his requirements. He ate a *lot*. Six eggs for breakfast, half a pound of bacon, and a triple stack of pancakes just to get him out the door. He drank two gallons of milk a day and water, more water than she could even measure. Lunches were about the same, large quantities of meat, and he could shovel pasta as if it were candy. The more he worked, the more he ate. It was understandable.

He called it carbo-loading. At night though, he usually ate little more than a salad with a side of chicken, and for snacks, he drank protein shakes.

Any normal person either would faint dead away or lecture him on the sins of gluttony or eating healthier. But she understood, at least for the most part, that he needed to put back what he used, and as he explained it to her, he wasn't about to show up to camp out of shape and flabby. Therefore, he ate and he worked out, constantly.

Alicia had apparently put up with it because she was looking for something bigger. Getting a sane person not wanting to be the first Mrs. Ironman was damned near impossible. He knew that.

Of course, he knew that. That's why he'd grinned that shit-eater grin of his at her when he'd put the condition on her leaving. She had to do the impossible; until then she stayed, and she took pity on him and cooked for him.

Asshole. Dickwad.

"Jerk!"

That was Thursday night; she hadn't spoken to him once since. She waited on Friday and Saturday for him to leave—without scrambling one single egg, thank you very much—before she went downstairs to start her daily routine. Check in with Sam, log into the team email account to see if any changes had occurred. Synchronize the two together and see what wouldn't work. Call Sam back see if he could get a reschedule on the

Gatorade commercial. Call the airline for a first-class ticket to New York. Text Jaime, wait for him to approve everything. Call Sam back and email him Jaime's itinerary including the trip to New York.

Then and only then did she go to the kitchen where she leisurely prepared herself breakfast: an egg, two slices of bacon—okay, three, because she really liked bacon—a slice of toast, and a bowl of strawberries, and milk. Jaime had convinced her that she needed the calcium now, while she was still in her twenties.

When he came in from his early-morning run along the beach, she smiled from beside the pool while he scrambled his own damned eggs. This, she thought, as she paddled her feet in the warm salt water, she could get used to. Maybe Jaime was right; she shouldn't leave. Why should she, when she had everything she needed without lifting a finger to get it.

On Sunday, she lay in bed until the ungodly

hour of ten o'clock. Jaime would have come back from his run by now, done his laps in the pool, and taken off for the team photo shoot that was scheduled for that afternoon. He wouldn't be back for lunch, so she had the whole day to herself.

She stretched, rolled out of bed, and decided that today was a good day to stay in her jammies. After a quick trip to the bathroom, she descended the stairs, her mouth minty fresh, her hair neatly pulled back in a sleek ponytail, only to stop dead in her tracks the second she entered the kitchen.

Jamison Dalton sat at the table dressed in little more than a towel, his face as gray and ominous as the storm that wailed beyond the row of French windows.

Her skin prickled when his golden gaze slowly caressed her body from the tips of her bare toes to her naked face, and every inch in between. Somehow she felt violated by the gleam in his eyes alone.

"So she is alive after all. I was beginning to

wonder." He sipped a glass of orange juice and leaned back in the chair, his well-formed, smooth-as-a-baby's-butt pectoral muscles flexing as he did. Aware that she was staring, and that he wanted her to stare, she sucked in her breath, squared her shoulders, and walked past him to the refrigerator, where she helped herself to a glass of the same juice.

"I'm taking a day off. Besides, aren't you supposed to be up in Davie getting your picture taken?"

"Cancelled due to weather. Which you would know, if you'd done your job."

"So I can't have one day all to myself? In the — what has it been now? — five weeks I've been here, I've not had one whole day to do what I want to do. It's called a day off; maybe you've heard of them?"

"And you thought you'd parade around here in sexy lingerie?"

"This is sexy? It's a cotton nightgown and …

and … and you're sitting over there naked under that towel, aren't you?" She felt her face turn red, completely red all the way to her hair. Of course, he was naked, she could see his trunks on the patio, and his hair was still dripping from his swim and the dash to get out of the storm. "You hate dripping water in from the pool, and you haven't been upstairs to shower yet."

"We're not talking about me. We're talking about you and that I pay you to take care of me and my needs, and my needs have not been met in three days now." He twitched his lips into that smile that she hated, sort of a half-smile in which he looked smug and condescending all at once. It was his debate smile when he thought he'd won.

"Wait a minute. You didn't actually hire me to do anything for you but liaison between you and your overfilled schedule. I volunteered out of the goodness of my heart to take care of your other needs. Wait, that sounds dirty. Oh wait, wait, I'm not taking care of any needs at all. Not even basic needs, and if you're thinking of anything else, I'm definitely not taking care of any of those needs, period."

"And out of the goodness of your heart, I'd like you to make breakfast. You at least make decent eggs." Did he really just order her to do something with a smile on his face?

"Uh, let me think about it for a moment." She plucked a packet of yogurt from the dairy drawer, and grabbing a spoon, she leaned on the counter to eat her breakfast. "That would be a no. I'll toss you a thingy of yogurt if you'd like; there's cereal in the pantry if you don't. Or, I don't know … cook your own damn eggs."

"That's my food you're eating. And you sleep in the room I provide and the clothes you wear … okay, I don't think I paid for that ugly thing."

"Okay, fine." She dropped the yogurt in the trash. "You want to play that game?

Fine, then I'll go to the store and buy my own food with the money you were supposed to put in my account for the work I did last month. Oh yeah, that check doesn't seem to be in the system yet. And I'll drive the car that you contractually are obligated to provide me until my services are terminated, in case you decide I can't even have that little luxury. And I will move out just as soon as that aforementioned paycheck for the last five weeks actually turns up."

His eyes narrowed, he pressed his lips into a thin line that sent shivers down her spine. Golden light sparked from behind lashes that were only a slightly darker shade. He looked like the devil incarnate, and her blood began to boil. Whether with fear or excitement she didn't know.

"Do you know what your problem is, Miss Pendleton?"

"So it's back to Miss Pendleton, then. What happened to Pepper? And Lord forbid you actually call me by my real name," she taunted him, watching in fascination as he leaned forward on one elbow and placed his chin in his hand. Did he know that he looked like a rippling, glowing, golden god when he moved like that?

Of course, he knew. Otherwise, he wouldn't move like that.

"You need a good spanking. That mouth of yours is out of control." His lips stretched into that sinful grin that reminded her of an animal on the prowl. He was toying with her, she knew that, biding his time before he went for the kill. Jamison Dalton was a master tormentor. She'd fallen into his trap too many times to count. One wrong move and she was toast, she knew that from experience.

"You aren't man enough to try that, *Mr. Dalton.*" Wrong move. Oh Jesus Christ, she knew to the very millisecond when Jaime Dalton decided to accept her challenge. All she could hope for now was to make it up the stairs and into her room before he could …

"Oh, fuck."

* * * * *

Jaime smiled. Her vain attempt at evading him was amusing. She had the deer-in-the-headlights look as he lunged from the chair at her taunt. Then she ran, at least she tried to run for the hall, but he zigged that way first, cutting her off. She stood staring at him, her chest heaving, her eyes wild but calculating. She looked from left to right just before she started for the other side of the island. Again, he anticipated her move, cutting off her escape.

"Nice try, babe, but remember, I play what amounts to a very violent game of tag for a living. I'm bigger than you, faster than you, and I have the home-field advantage."

"But I'm smarter than you," she shot back as she eased toward the patio doors, then feinted back to the island once she drew him away.

"Not so much." Blood pumped in his brain, the thrill of the chase blinding him to everything but catching Cass Pendleton and making her pay for all of the little slights and insults he'd endured over the past few weeks. And after everything he'd done for her too.

"Why are you doing this?"

That was a loaded question he had no intention of answering.

"Fine, then. I'll take my chances in the rain."

He caught her just as she reached the grill area and grabbed her around her waist.

She screamed a blood-curdling scream that made his blood race even faster.

She kicked, clawed, and called him names he wouldn't have guessed she knew the meaning of. But he didn't let her go. Instead he found the jump rope he'd left out the day before, and with one hand he held her arms behind her back, with the other he cinched her elbows together and wound the rope a couple of times, finally tying it in a bow.

Cass stopped struggling immediately. She stood stone still, staring at him with mayhem in her eyes. "Not funny, Jaime. Let me go. Let me go now and I won't kill you."

"Pretty talk. You should be on your knees, begging me to let you go instead of making threats you aren't in a position to carry out." He noticed that her breath grew ragged, but murder still shone brightly in her eyes. "I'll let you go when you learn to speak to me with a civil tongue. Yes, Mr. Dalton or Lord Ironman—either is acceptable.

Yes, Mr. Dalton. Do you think you can manage that, Miss Pendleton?"

"Go fuck yourself." She stood tall, her shoulders forced back, her breasts jutting against the pulled tight material of her gown that was little more than a long, sleeveless T-shirt, her nipples hard as pebbles.

Something stirred inside him, a beast he thought he'd long ago shackled, when it came to Cassandra Pendleton and her mouth. Her perfectly formed full red lips—oh so perfect for kissing, but very adept at spewing vile, hateful words. Words that had made him want to do dishonorable things to her for as long as he could remember.

"Maybe later. Right now, Miss Pendleton, I believe I owe you a spanking." He slowly walked around her, touching her shoulder, her upper arms, stroking her cheek as he circled her, dragging out the torment. "Not quite so mouthy now, are you? How do you want it? Leaning across the table or my lap?"

She didn't answer; she just stood still and watched him, with something akin to hatred in her eyes. He didn't like the sick feeling in his stomach those looks caused.

However, instead of untying her and running for his life, he decided it was a good idea to cover her eyes with the forgotten dishtowel that lay on the table beside the grill. "I'm sorry, Miss Pendleton, but you brought this on yourself. And if it's any consolation, this is going to hurt you more than it hurts me."

She started to reply, but he cinched the cloth around her eyes, and the words she had been about to say became a breathy gasp. "Now, Miss Pendleton, I'm going to give you one chance to apologize for all of the mean things you say to me." The rise and fall of her chest was mesmerizing, her pointed nipples seemed to beckon him to touch. Jaime cleared his throat.

"Let me go." Her voice was soft, breathy, disconcerting.

"Apologize or get spanked." Why didn't he just let her go?

"No. I won't." She drew in her breath when he twined his fingers in her hair; the long thick ponytail felt like silk. He pulled her head back and leaned in. He could feel her breath on his cheek. It was minty and sweet, he could see the wild fluttering of her pulse at the base of her neck, and before he could stop himself, he picked her up and carried her back into the house.

She felt like a rag doll in his arms, limp, pliable, and oh so soft. "Then you leave me no other choice."

He pulled the chair nearest the doorway out with his foot and settled on it. Shifting her until she lay across his legs, he lifted her gown to bare her bottom. "Last chance." He stifled the moan that clogged his throat. The white lace panties she wore hugged her ass cheeks, leaving the lower globes bare and almost begging him to touch.

"No." Her words were faint, whispered, almost as if she wanted him to ... She yelped when he swatted her left cheek. Not hard, just enough to sting his palm.

"Say, 'I'm sorry, Mr. Dalton.'"

"No," she whimpered against his leg when he swatted her right cheek.

"I'm sorry, Mr. Dalton." He didn't wait for her to answer before bringing his hand down on her smooth ass cheeks again, and then a second time. As he watched, a faint damp spot began to show. A third time, and if he wasn't sure of it, her whispered use of his name convinced him even further. Cassandra Pendleton was turned on.

"Does this turn you on, Miss Pendleton?" He smacked her again, first one cheek, then the other, ending each with a caress.

"No," she gasped after the second slap, the damp spot growing darker with each contact.

"Then why are you wet down here?"

"Jaime, please," Cass almost moaned when he laid his hand across her legs just below her crotch.

"Please, Jaime, what? More? Do you want more, Pepper?" She shook her head, her long hair swishing the floor. He touched her, just lightly, in the center of the damp spot, and she grew very still, her breathing became shallow.

"Do you want to be touched here?" He stroked the cloth lightly. She was hot and oh so wet; he almost moaned with her.

"No." But she didn't sound very convincing. "Please, Jaime."

"Please, Jaime, what? Tell me what you want, Pepper."

"More," she whimpered, he could hear the

self-loathing in her voice. Cassandra Pendleton wanted him to touch her, in that way. "Oh God."

"Okay." He lifted the small strip of sodden fabric and with great difficulty, wiggled it down her legs until she lay bare-assed across his legs, her damp flesh begging him to touch and to taste and to take. He controlled the last urge and slid an exploratory finger along the moist lips. Her groan was all the invitation he needed to go deeper.

She called his name, her voice a pleading whisper. She wanted more. He was on the verge of losing control.

Instead of going deeper, instead of leaning over just that small fraction it would take to know what she tasted like, he lowered her to the floor, steadying her on her knees. She whimpered, squeezing her legs together.

"Spread your legs, Pepper." He didn't really expect her to do as he said, but to his surprise, she did. He leaned back in the chair, in stunned disbelief. "Pull your shoulders back and lift your head up, show me your tits."

Her lips pulled into a thin line, noting her displeasure at the request, but just when Jaime decided he'd imagined her acquiescence, she did as he ordered. Amazing.

Pepper liked it kinky. His cock throbbed at the knowledge. Christ, Cassandra Pendleton was trussed up like a Christmas goose on his kitchen floor. He was going straight to hell. He just knew it.

"You have beautiful breasts, Pepper," he felt obligated to tell her. "Nice and round, just enough to fit in my hands."

He knelt before her as he spoke, and tilted her chin up with his finger. Her lips were soft when he brushed his thumbs across them, easing her mouth open. "I love your hair.

I've always wanted to know what it felt like." He pulled the elastic band out and let her hair fall over the blindfold. "Beautiful."

"I'm going to touch you now. Lean back for

me, touch the floor with your fingers." She did, bending her back until her breasts jutted high and proud against her chest. Her mouth fell slack when he cupped her, small whimpering sounds escaped with each light flick of his thumbs across her painfully hard nipples.

"Pepper, this is so, oh God, this is…" He couldn't help himself, he tugged her gown up and over her head, letting it catch on the rope binding her arms together.

"Nasty," she finished for him.

"Exactly." His cock throbbed painfully, begging for release. He ignored it as he studied her body with his eyes and hands. Finding sensitive spots that made her purr or gasp, and when he finally slipped his finger between the lightly hair-covered lower lips, she shuddered violently. When her first orgasm passed, she said the one word that he knew he couldn't ignore.

"More."

He moved behind her and pressed his body to

her, molding to her curves. He ran his hands down her body, starting with her breasts, massaging her until she began to pant with need. He pressed his erection into her hands and nearly cried out when she gripped him tight.

"That's nice, Pepper, stroke me," he ordered her as he slid one finger between her legs, past her throbbing clit, until he was buried inside her. "That's right, baby, just like that."

He set the rhythm, adding a second finger, then a third, while he rocked into her hand. He felt her orgasm begin deep inside. The slick walls clenched him tight, her hands on his cock became more insistent. She called out his name, but he didn't hear her for the blood rushing in his ears from the force of his own release.

When it was over, all he could think to do was pull the rope free and whisper a hasty apology, before he retreated upstairs like the coward he really was.

* * * * *

Cass lay on the cold tile floor, waiting for feeling to return to her arms; cold penetrated her bare flesh. She knew she was alone. Shame prickled her scalp, but she didn't raise a hand to shake off the loose rope or to remove the blindfold. Something warm and sticky soaked her gown where it lay against her back.

After a few moments, the floor became uncomfortable and humiliation set in. She sat up, leaving the rope behind, and dragged the cloth from her eyes. Strange lightning stung her eyes and then ceased abruptly. She glanced out at the abating storm, then in a fit of absolute horror, she grabbed her panties off the floor, and clutching her sticky gown to her chest, she raced upstairs and locked the door. But that didn't still her racing heart or her screaming mind.

She wanted to hate him. To pack her bags and catch the first flight out of Miami; she didn't really care where it went as long as he wasn't on it. Instead, she hated herself because she'd liked what he'd done. She hated herself because even now she had the strongest urge to find him and beg for more.

But she knew in her heart that this could never happen again. Even if she didn't leave. This could never happen again or else a part of her very being would be lost.

Forever.

Chapter Nine

Monday morning dawned bright and sunny, what coastal people called beach weather. Cass considered skipping her usual morning routine and walking down to the beach and standing knee deep in the surf.

She didn't want to risk an encounter with Jaime today, not after avoiding him after the events of yesterday morning. However, the Pollyanna she really was deep inside reared her ugly head and demanded she go and do her actual job. She dressed in walking shorts and a three-quarter-length-sleeved peasant blouse in a startling crimson color and matching sandals. She quickly braided her hair in a loose over the shoulder braid and didn't bother with makeup.

She really didn't expect him to be home, but as

she neared his office, she heard his voice. He sounded angry. The door was open, and she stepped inside to find him on the phone, his expression pinched. He signaled for her to be quiet but not to leave. She gulped, wondering if he planned to turn his anger onto her.

"So, Cam, let me get this straight. You said you transferred the funds to Miss Pendleton's account each Friday as I asked you too. And the June bills as well. Yes, I'm aware that my credit card bill was incredibly high. I put my entire signing bonus into that account, there should be plenty of money to cover one month's worth of bills. Really? I deposited that back in early May. Yes, I bought a car, and my trip to France was luxurious. The jewelry was returned. I don't see how that's any of your business. Miss Pendleton says she has yet to receive a single deposit. Of course I believe her." He looked at her, then fire lit his golden eyes. She knew him well enough by now to know that she was grateful she wasn't in this Cam guy's shoes.

"Of course Miss Pendleton doesn't have access to that account; only you and I have access, and I know for a fact that I haven't spent two million dollars since the first of May. Cam, do you really think I'm so stupid as to put all of my money into one account.

I'm not broke, son, but I'm sure the money will turn up before the audit my lawyer is preparing as we speak. Of course, Cam. I understand. Expect a call within the hour. Sure thing, and you take care too."

He pressed a button and started speaking again. "Did you get that Mitch?, Yeah, today. No, Cameron and Associates only handles my fun money." He paused, looking through an address index and rattling off four different accounting firms. "Cam only has access to a couple at a time. No, I don't trust him. I don't trust any of them, that's why. It might be only a couple of million, but it's my couple of million. I'm the one wrecking my body for that money, not some fat bald accountant. Do what you have to—some jail time if it comes to that. Yeah, man, and sorry to stick you with this so early in the morning… You too."

She waited this time for him to put the phone down. "Is there a problem?"

"Not really, thanks to you. Oh and here." He handed her a check for an obscene amount of money. "Sorry it's so late."

"I, ah, okay. Jaime?" She had no idea what she wanted to say to him or hear from him.

He turned quizzical eyes on her and waited for her to say something. When she didn't, he rose from the chair and walked around. "I'm late. I'm going to be up in Davie all day today if you need me. And don't forget that you start at the Boys and Girls Club this afternoon." He looked as if he wanted to say more—and did she imagine that he reached for her arm, but pulled back as if she might burn him? "And Pepper, you look nice this morning."

Before she could reply, he was gone. She sat in his chair, which was still warm from his presence, and just as she reached for the phone, it rang. Sam had grown impatient and couldn't wait to tell someone that the trip to New York needed to be extended because he got Jaime a Nike deal. She told him to call Jaime on his cell so he could tell him himself.

She checked Jaime's schedule, noticed that he had already initialed the daily calendar so he didn't need her to text him today. Feeling at loose ends, she started to leave the office when the phone rang again.

"Hey, did you hear? Sam got me a Nike deal. We've been after one for three years.   Guess that finally means I'm somebody, huh? Pepper, are you there?"

"Yeah, Jaime, that's great. How long are you going to be in New York so I can change your ticket?"

"A week, maybe a couple days longer, I don't

know right now, Sam said he'll call tonight with a final schedule. And Pepper, I … ah … get yourself a ticket too. I'm going to be gone too long; I might need you."

"You want me to go to New York with you?" Why did her heart rate just spike?

"Yeah, who else would I take? And Pepper … time to pull out those boutique clothes, and don't forget a cocktail dress. There's a reception at The Plaza. And…"

"I don't have anything nice enough to wear to The Plaza and … and … wouldn't you rather take a date or one of your girlfriends? Why me?"

"Why not you? If you think you don't have anything nice enough, then go shopping.   Get something blue. I like the way your eyes look in blue." He hung up on her. That son of a bitch was laughing. If she didn't know better she would swear he'd had this all planned from the beginning.

"Jerk," she shouted at the phone receiver.

Before she put it down, she dialed the airline to change the tickets. Then without thinking, she called the spa and asked to speak with Shontal. He would know the best place in Miami to buy a fancy blue dress. While she was on the phone, he scheduled her for another appointment.

Oh Lord, they were going to rip hair out of tender places again. However, this time that didn't seem so bad.

*****

Why he thought taking Pepper to New York would be fun, he never knew. But she looked lovely for the flight. Her hair was sleek and lustrous, and she was dressed in navy blue Capri pants, another of her peasant-style blouses, this one silk with elaborate embroidery at the neckline, and a pair of low-heeled wedge shoes with straps that wrapped around her ankles.

The only visible sign of her nervousness was her hands. She couldn't stop shaking. He took her hand on takeoff, held her tight, and leaned against her so only she could hear him murmur stupid nonsense things about anything he could think of.

When the flight leveled out and the seat belt sign went off, Pepper relaxed, but only a little. She twined her fingers with his, her grip surprisingly strong. "Breathe, Pepper. You're doing fine. Just breathe and relax."

"I am breathing." Her words were clipped, anxious.

"No, you are hyperventilating," he said just as the flight attendant approached, pushing her cart. Her eyes widened as she recognized him, her gaze going to his hand linked with Pepper's. "Miss, can I get a glass of champagne for Miss Pendleton, and I'd like a Coke if you have one."

"Anything, Mr. Dalton." Tall and blonde, with intelligent blue eyes, she was just his type. Too bad she'd sized the situation with Pepper up completely wrong. "Is she all right?"

Pepper had closed her eyes and was counting

aloud; her fingernails, digging into his hand, were sharp. "First time flying commercial. I'm hoping the booze calms her down before she has a heart attack."

"In that case, here, take two." She handed the flutes of champagne over to him along with the Coke and pushed past as if she thought Pepper would combust at any moment.

"Here, Pepper, drink." He pressed the golden liquid into her hand and watched as she upended it, draining it in one gulp. "Okay, now?"

"Better." She said releasing the pressure on his hand, but not altogether. After the second drink, she relaxed completely, her words were slightly slurred, and she smiled up at him a lot. Her eyes shone from the wine. "You know, Jaime, you really are a nice-looking man, despite your bad attitude. It's no wonder all of the women stop and stare at you. Some of the men too."

"I guess you're right, Pepper, but I am mildly famous too, you know."

"Really? What for?"

"Pepper, are you drunk?" He couldn't help laughing when she reached for his hand and missed. "You *are* drunk. It was only two glasses, Pepper."

"I know. I can't handle it. You should know that by now."

"Are you going to puke?" He remembered that first morning they'd spent together.

Her leaning over the toilet, topless, spilling all of the gin and most of her dinner into the toilet, and him fighting an erection and a serious feeling of foreboding.

"Not right now. I could sleep, though. I didn't get much last night." Her eyes were drooping, now that she pointed it out. "Do I have time for a nap?"

"About four hours. Give or take."

"Oh good." She laid her head on his shoulder, and before he could react, her breathing turned soft and rhythmic. He didn't have the heart to tumble her back in her own seat, so he let her be, flying the entire nonstop trip holding Cassandra Pendleton's hand while she slept, and ignoring the overly invasive looks of the other passengers and flight staff as well.

Tomorrow there would be a gossip item somewhere about his non-relationship with his personal assistant. He would deal with that tomorrow; for now he simply enjoyed watching her sleep and the blessed silence that went along with it.

Mercy Celeste

Chapter Ten

About three days into her stay at the Plaza with Jaime Dalton, Cass came to one horrific realization. Jaime didn't drink. Ever. However, he sure as hell didn't mind getting her buzzed if it suited his purposes. And tonight it seemed to suit his purpose.

He looked magnificent in a tuxedo, with his blond hair slicked back from his face, a diamond ring glittering on his ring finger—his team ring, he'd told her. He'd also told her that after this year he expected to replace it with a Super Bowl ring. He was deadly serious, but she didn't understand anything he said after that.

"You don't speak football, do you, Pepper?" he asked after her second glass of wine.

The Nike reception had turned into a full-out

party in the Plaza ballroom. Loud music played, and big men and beautiful women danced around them. "That's all right, you look great in that dress, and that's all that matters."

"I know two things, Jaime Dalton, about football." She liked the way he looked at her when he said she looked great in that dress. As if he were trying to think of a way to get her out of it. And since that morning last week, she hadn't been able to think of anything but getting naked with him. Often. Excessively often. Like in the middle of lunch today, when he offered her a bite of his sandwich and his fingers brushed her lips, and she thought she might melt.

"What's that, Pepper?" He smiled at her, his eyes sparkling in the dim lights. She knew that look. He used it when he thought he was messing with her head.

"That you play it, and that I'm not interested in it."

"At least you have that much down pat."

Something about him was slightly off. He laughed too often, talked too loud, and looked around too much.

"Jaime, are you looking for someone?" she asked after her third glass of wine disappeared. She didn't actually remember drinking it. But she felt all nice and ... fuzzy.

"No. Hey, Pepper, you want to dance?" He didn't wait for her to respond before he dragged her to her feet and into the middle of the group of people who were doing little more than rubbing their bodies together.

"This isn't dancing," she told him sometime into the second song after he mashed her chest to his.

"Then what do you call it?" He looped her hands behind his neck and swayed with her.

"I don't know. Are you hard?" There was a definite bulge pressed against her belly.

"You look very nice tonight. That dress fits you perfectly," was his answer. His breath against her cheek was warm. "Are you wearing another pair of those cheeky panties you like?"

"Are you flirting with me? No, seriously, I can't tell—either you are flirting or being mean. Which is it?"

"Flirting, I guess," he sighed, his eyes growing distant. "Failing too."

"Not really. I just wanted to make sure I was reading you right. Besides, I want you to. Flirt, not be mean. I'm tired of fighting with you."

"Then you won't mind if I do this." He placed his hand on her ass and squeezed, pressing her closer as he did so. The bulge behind his tuxedo trousers grew harder, larger, causing her to gasp.

"I was hoping you would kiss me, but I guess that's okay too."

"Pepper." He stared into her eyes, flame raging behind his whiskey-colored eyes, warning her that playing with him was definitely playing with fire. "I'm going to take you upstairs now. If you have any objections, you might want to say something."

"Will there be bondage and spanking involved?"

"If you want." He stopped stone still, as if he were holding his breath waiting for her to reply.

"Did I say I did?" She wasn't that drunk. But her heart rate did spike at the thought.

"I was hoping for a little revenge from last week."

"Oh, then you want to tie me up and spank me?"

"The thought occurred to me."

"No, absolutely not."

"Like you gave me a choice."

"You liked it."

"Maybe I did, maybe I didn't."

"You liked it, Pepper. You were cream beneath my hand. I could have done anything to you, and you would have begged for more."

She noticed belatedly that he was slowly leading her to the edge of the dance floor, almost casually, trying not to call attention to them and their quiet argument. So what if he was right. She'd wanted him to bend her over and fill her from behind. Craved it the whole time he finger fucked her, his cock hard and huge in her hand, when it should have been inside her.

"Why are we discussing this now? I thought you were avoiding the issue?"

"I was, but now that we're talking about it, I've got this profound urge to…"

"You are not tying me up again, Jaime Dalton." But even as she hissed the words, her traitorous body began to tingle in all the wrong spots.

"If you don't want me to, then why are your nipples hard and your breathing ragged?" He smiled that Cheshire cat smile at her, and she knew the game was becoming dangerous.

"Because this dress is irritating my skin, because we're dancing, because you're doing that thing you do when you try to get me off balance and embarrass myself."

"All I'm doing is walking you to the elevator. In case you didn't notice, we left the dance floor a while ago."

"Then why am I still pressed against you?"

"Because I like you there. And because it keeps you off balance so I can do this." As she watched, he loosened his tie and slid it from around his neck. The silk material was still warm from his body when he wrapped it around her arms, just above her elbows and pulled it tight.

"People can see," she hissed, anger and fear once again filling her senses. "And you don't want the media to know about me."

"They already know about you, Pepper."

"They know I'm your assistant. You think I haven't noticed that I embarrass you.

You certainly would rather they don't find out you have some sort of kinky need to tie me up because you can't dominate me any other way."

"Keep it up and I'll gag you," he said just as

the elevator doors opened. Thankfully, no one emerged to overhear them. Or worse, to see her arms tied behind her back. "Is this scarf thing around your neck pinned or anything?"

"No, why?" She watched in horror as he tugged the long silk scarf from the elaborate knot and pulled it from around her neck. "No, Jaime, please don't." But it was too late, the elevator went dark, and she heard him chuckle.

"Why is it when I cover your eyes, you stop talking?" He ran his hand along her arm, over her shoulder. Goose bumps followed everywhere he touched. "It is a miracle. Oh, Pepper, your hair smells wonderful."

She liked his fingers in her hair; the way he ran them through the strands felt sinful.

"Are you wearing a bra?"

"No," she whispered against his cheek, the elevator wall cold beneath her back. He had fast hands. He tugged her skirt up, caressing her leg with one, while the other stroked her throat.

"I love these panties. Damn, Pepper, how many pairs do you have?" He cupped her ass, running a finger under the lace.

"I don't know. Several."

"At least you have good taste in something," he said just before he slapped her there, caressing after she yelped. "We've got five more floors to go, baby. Think I can make you moan before then?"

She didn't have time to answer, he slid his finger down her back crack, between her legs, and before she could catch her breath, he pushed into her, sliding in just deep enough to make her wet—not that she needed much coaxing—then out to torment her clit. She wanted more, deeper—oh God, his cock felt huge against her belly, and she arched against him. "That's it baby; oh that feels good. Can you come for me, Pepper? Right here in the elevator."

He eased his other hand between her legs, pushing her back against the wall as he surrounded her, filling her from behind with one, stroking her clit from the front with the other. "Come for me, Pepper. Oh yeah, that's my girl."

She couldn't stop it, the double onslaught more than she could handle. Sensation swirled inside her, from her toes to the tips of her hair, consuming her. His jacket was rough against her face; she cried his name against his shoulder begging him to stop, begging for more, until she lost herself completely, and the world came to a sudden spinning halt.

"Our floor." He withdrew his fingers from her slick pussy, her dress slithering down her leg made her gasp just as the doors slid open.

As he took her by her elbow and walked her down the hall, she could feel his impatience.

Thank God they weren't far from the elevator; she didn't think she would manage to stay upright much longer. Her legs shook, as did her arms. Her skin felt super sensitive where he touched her. The slightest graze of his jacket or his pants leg had her trembling with anticipation and need, so much so, that by the time he closed the door to their suite behind them, she was on the verge of melting.

"How do I take this dress off?" He leaned her against the door while he fumbled with the straps that crossed her back.

"It zips at the side, but you'll have to untie me to take it off."

"Fuck that, I don't have that much time." She heard a sickening rip and knew the delicate lace didn't survive his big hands, but she didn't care. His mouth on her nipple was hot, the air on her skin cool. "Oh God, Pepper, you taste good. Like vanilla ice cream. I could spend the rest of my life tasting you."

She didn't know how to respond to that, but the groan that came out must have pleased him because he picked her up, and before she could count to three, she was lying on her stomach in the middle of a bed of silk. Her bed. It had to be, his was at the far back of the suite. "And as much as I like these, they have to go." He pulled her panties down her legs and over one sandal, then the other, catching on the heel of the second one before he tugged it off. "The sandals can stay. Get on your knees, Pepper."

His hand stung when he struck her — once, twice — pain and need swimming through her mind at the same time. "Spread your legs," he ordered. "I want to see your pussy. That's it. Pepper, spread them wide. Just for me. Mmm, Pepper, you have a pretty pussy."

"Jaime?" She didn't know why she called his name, she hated him, but God, she wanted him to touch her. She'd do anything if he would touch her. There, right there.

His tongue was so damned hot she had to bury her face in the comforter to keep from screaming when he licked her clit. "So sweet. You have a sweet pussy, Pepper." She couldn't stop this time; she cried out, his name, God's name. Her toes felt like they were on fire as he licked her, flicking her clit with his teeth. "Oh baby, scream for me. I like that."

She mourned the loss of his tongue, the heat, the sudden plummet back to earth from the brim of insanity. Hypersensitive to everything, sound, scent, touch, she felt him move onto the bed behind her, heard the soft sound of something tearing and then the zinging sound of his zipper.

"Open for me, Pepper. Oh yeah, baby, that's it; tell me how you like that." The blunt head of his cock eased into her slowly — agonizingly slow. "How does that feel, Pepper?" he asked again, drawing her mind down from the stratosphere, forcing her to acknowledge him, and the things he did to her.

"Jaime." She had no idea how to tell him how good it felt, she tilted her hips to take him deeper. His moan when she eased back against him told her all she needed to know.

* * * * *

Pleasure, hot, wet, and greedy, enfolded him. Dark hair and honey golden flesh tumbled against chocolate silk inflamed him. Her strangled cries sent him reeling. Her skin gleamed in the light, sweat-sheened and as silky as the spread beneath her.

Her face was a mask of pleasure and pain as he pressed into her; her hands lay against her sides, useless, her fingers reaching for the bed or for him, unable to reach either. She shifted on her knees, angling her body to take him deeper, her ass smooth beneath his hands as he grasped her, guiding her back against him. Her creamy pussy throbbed around him, driving him to do things and say things he'd never dared before.

Cassandra Pendleton took him to the edge of sanity. Her cries for more and harder, faster were more than he could bear. She spiraled over that edge, her body contracting around him, threatening to take him with her. But he wasn't nearly ready to lose himself.

There was so much more of Cass to taste. He wanted to taste every square inch before the night was over.

He fought orgasm, waiting for the one gripping her to pass before he eased out, untying her arms as he went. She reached for the blindfold, but he grabbed her arms and flipped her onto her back. "Leave it," he told her. "Or I'll tie you to the headboard."

"I want to touch you." Her words were not much more than a sob.

"Leave the blindfold on and I'll let you touch me."

"All right," she said with a sigh as she stretched her hands.

"Do your arms hurt?" He was sorry for that. The last thing he wanted to do was hurt her.

"They tingle, some."

"Don't lie to me, Pepper. Do your arms hurt?"

"Yes, it hurts when you tie me like that."

"But you like it anyway. Don't lie. You're not a very good liar."

"Yes. I like when you tie me up. I like when

you spank me. It makes me…"

"What?" Her jaw turned stubborn and she sighed, but she didn't answer. "It makes you what?"

"Horny, all right? You make me so Goddamned horny, I hate you."

"But you'd do anything I ask, wouldn't you?"

She didn't answer; she drew her mouth into a thin line. The Cass he knew and barely tolerated was threatening to return. So he rolled her onto her side, and before he even knew what he was about to do, he smacked her ass. "Answer me. You'd do anything I ask, Pepper, wouldn't you?" He hit her again, the small intake of breath followed by the yelp of pain threatened to undo his hard fought for control.

"Yes, I like when you spank me, Jaime. I'll do anything you ask. Please, do it again."

"Would you go down on me in public?" He had no idea why he asked her that. Just to see if she would answer. Hell, he didn't even know if she'd go down on him in private yet. He followed the request with another slap to her red-mottled bottom.

"Yes."

"Shit, Pepper. You really shouldn't give me that kind of ammunition. I just might use it."

"Then why did you ask me to?"

"To see if you'd answer me. Christ, Pepper, would you really … Goddamn, that makes me…"

"Makes you what? Jaime, damn it. Makes you what?"

He wanted to say happy, but that would just be giving her something to use against him. Instead, he rolled her onto her back again and tugged her legs up, spreading her wide. "It makes me horny, baby. Get ready. I'm going to make you scream again."

* * * * *

He still wore his shirt when he entered her. She fumbled with the studs as she searched for skin. When she finally found it, she almost cried out.

His mouth found hers, finally, his lips scorching, demanding that she open for him; his tongue, at first harsh, invaded her mouth, and then he groaned, grinding into her, slowly, his pelvic bone sharp against hers. She gave him her tongue; he greedily suckled it as he lifted her shoulders, tucking his arms beneath her until she felt engulfed by him.

"That's it, baby," he whispered next to her ear when she twined her arms around his back, and stroked him, going lower until she clasped his hard-muscled ass cheeks in her hands. "That feels good. Come for me, Pepper."

His breath was harsh against her ear, his chest hot against hers, his cock hard and throbbing inside as he slowly rode her. His very words inflamed her. "Come for me, baby." God, she wanted to hold him like this forever. His hard body fit perfectly to hers; he moved fluidly inside her, engulfed her, inflamed her. She could feel him, the long hard length of him gliding inside her, touching that spot that she didn't know existed, that spot that made her want to do everything he asked. "Pepper." His breath turned shallow, his thrusts became slower, deeper.

"Jaime, I'm there, now, I..." There wasn't anything to say; sensation took over. He growled, almost animal-like, and pain shot through her shoulder—sharp, biting pain that sent her zooming past the atmosphere. Still he held her imprisoned by his mouth and his body pumping into her harder, faster until she ceased to exist.

"Pepper," she heard him roar, and then she fell back to earth, shattered, broken into a trillion little pieces. And that's how she stayed for a very long time.

Mercy Celeste

Chapter Eleven

"In two weeks my life is pretty much going to become one long session in hell," Jamie told her one morning, a week after New York, as she placed a plate of eggs and sausage in front of him. "I might not come home most nights, and if I do it will be late, and I'll just be back out the door, probably before you get up."

"Okay." Cass sat across from him at the table. It was odd to see him dressed in regular clothes and not wet or sweaty for a change. "Football camp, right?"

"Yeah, two weeks of hell, and then the preseason starts. Practice is open to the public if you want to drive up one afternoon. When you're not at the school, of course."

"Maybe, if I can find time. I joined a book

club, and I signed up for a cooking class."

"Good. It's nice that you're keeping busy. If you want to come and watch, just let me know and I'll get you a pass."

"I'll let you know." She watched him over her coffee cup. He looked everywhere but directly at her. It had been like this since the morning after at the Plaza. He'd slept with her, made love to her in the wee hours of morning, and then nothing. It was as if it never happened. "What are your plans for today?"

"I have a meeting with Mitch. That fuck Cameron is being difficult. He stole nearly two million dollars from me, or he is covering for one of his lackeys. The court has ordered an audit, and today is the day. My receipts against their books. Thank God, Alicia's check cleared before he cleaned me out, or that would be one more pile of crap I'd have to wade through."

"Can I ask if you're all right financially without sounding too much like a gold digger?"

"Well, you just did, and yeah, you sound sort of gold-diggerish. Really, Pepper, Nike just paid me ten million to look sweaty and pretty in their commercials for the next year.

That is only one of my endorsements. Plus, there is my actual salary and investments to consider. Let's just say I can keep you in sexy panties for a very long time. What Cam mislaid, shall we say, is nothing; don't worry about it."

"You know that's the first time…" She didn't know how to bring it up. Something had changed between them since that night. He avoided her, and when he was in the same room with her it was like this, all polite conversation, and it was driving her crazy. "Are you going to ever acknowledge what happened between us?"

"Why? Unless you're interested in going upstairs with me, I don't see a reason to. It happened. It was bound to happen. Do you want it to happen again?" He looked at her, finally, but his eyes didn't hold any of the usual fire.

"Not really. But I can't help but wonder where we go from here."

"Hell, Cass, I'm not marrying you, if that's what you're looking for. Just because I've seen you naked and sampled your goodies doesn't mean I want to set up house."

"Well, I don't like playing house with you either. This makes me tense. My stress level is through the roof. Living with you, doing everything for you. While you move my things around and rearrange the kitchen, which I don't appreciate, by the way. I might not be the best cook, but I like things to stay where I put them."

"Well, damn, Cass, get a hobby, because this is pretty much it. And for the last time, I'm not messing with your things."

"I have about fifty hobbies. And you're an ass."

"Gee, I think I preferred when you called me jerk."

"Oh fuck you."

"Fine, go get the jump rope."

"Weren't you late for something? Like your hanging."

"Now that's the Pepper I know and love." He smiled that smile, the one that told her he was back to normal, then he glanced at the clock over the stove. "Oh fuck, I really am late. See you tonight, Pepper. And wear something sexy, I'm taking you out to dinner; maybe we'll get in a little dancing."

His laughter echoed from the garage, and then he was gone. Well, at least he'd forgotten about asking her to do things to him in public. She hoped.

* * * * *

Over the next two weeks, Jaime watched her from as far away as he could. Pepper really did have too many hobbies. Besides going to the school every afternoon to read stories and volunteer as an English tutor, she went to a book club, a cooking class, and even though she had finished painting all the rooms in his house, she still liked to collect and refinish old furniture. He had to admit that a few of the pieces were beautiful when she found the perfect place for them.

Her current obsession was the dining room, or rather the lack thereof. She seemed determined to find pieces from the same era the house was built. After reading up on the history of the place and of that time period in Miami, even he had to admit more than just a passing interest.

She'd stopped talking of moving out, and after that one morning, she didn't seem interested in pursuing the topic of whatever this thing between them was or wasn't. Right now, he didn't have time for a thing with Cassandra Pendleton. He didn't want a thing with Cassandra Pendleton, but damned if he wanted Cassandra Pendleton to move into an apartment.

He liked the way she hummed when she cooked his eggs. He liked coming home at night to find her puttering in the garage, or the kitchen, or sitting out by the pool reading a book. He liked talking with her. About whatever she was doing, and answering her questions about his life and what exactly he did on the field. She had to be the single most disinterested woman in the history of football groupies. She knew nothing, not even what a quarterback did. Most people at least knew that much, but not Pepper. Of course, she never tuned him out when he wanted to talk about his day, as if his constant workouts and meal schedule was all that interesting. She listened, and that was more than he could remember anyone besides his parents doing.

After that morning, things got back to normal. She sniped at him. He sniped at her.

They went about their business and slept in their separate beds, just as it was meant to be.

Sometimes, especially when she wore a dress, he wondered what color her panties were.

He thought about those back to school essays

they used to write on the first day of school.

Well, he'd certainly shock some poor teacher if he had to sum up how he spent his summer vacation. Not only did he spend the bulk of his days thinking about the color of Cassandra Pendleton's cheeky panties; there were the off days when he spent his free time coming up with ingenious ways to get into her panties. Only to turn chickenshit at the last moment, all because Cassandra Pendleton looked at him with those smoky blue eyes and his entire world suddenly became more complicated. And he sure as hell did not need complicated in his life right now. That's when the first package arrived. Cass always left the mail on his desk.

Apparently, complicated now came in FedEx envelopes. He didn't recognize the return address but opened it anyway. After viewing the contents, he felt queasy. The accompanying letter left him downright nauseous. He filed the entire thing away in his safe, so that Cass couldn't find it, and made a mental note to hand the whole thing over to Mitch just as soon as he could figure out a way that wouldn't completely ruin him or Cass in the process.

Mercy Celeste

Chapter Twelve

A few days before Jaime was to leave for camp, Cass found him walking the perimeter of his property. He was acting strange; okay, stranger than usual. Up until now, she'd never seen him touch the plants that covered the brick wall that surrounded the property, but she really wouldn't call what he was doing gardening. It was more like he was searching for something. And he spent a great deal of time at the back gate that led to the trail down to the beach. He even had the security code changed on the lock.

Then there were the private, whispered calls to his lawyer to consider. The questions about the people she'd met during her daily trek about town. She had to swear on a stack of bibles that she'd never told anyone who she worked for, and that included deliverymen bringing in furniture and workers bringing in whatever they were doing.

"What's going on, Jaime?" She finally asked the Saturday before camp started, he was holding a FedEx package as if it might bite him, his face a sickening shade of pale.

"Nothing I can't handle, Cass," he said, but she knew the smile he flashed her was forced. Besides, he didn't call her Pepper, which by itself was enough to worry her. "Uh, how would you like to take one of those vacation weeks this week? I'll fly you anywhere you want to go, or you can go home and visit your Mom. This week is just going to be me at camp and you all alone here."

"I'm not really interested in going anywhere right now, and my mom went to Vegas with her Red Hat group. She said thanks, by the way, for sending her the money."

"I didn't send her any money."

"I know. I did; I just said it was from you

because she refused to take it when I offered. She wants me to start a retirement fund and open up a savings account and not spend money on frivolous things like trips to play the slots with a bunch of old ladies. But she has no qualms about spending your money."

"Your mom is hardly old. She's what, maybe fifty?"

"Forty-eight. She was twenty when I was born. My dad ran out on her a couple of months later, and well, she's never had much of a life. So if she wants to go gambling with a bunch of gray-hairs, then I say more power to her. Besides, after I paid off my debts, I don't have anything to spend my earnings on. Some groceries here and there, and Barnes and Noble is getting rich off of me, but after that…" She shrugged; she never liked to talk about how she grew up—not poor but not far from it. There was always food and everything she needed, but there was never anything extra, like trips down to the beach or anywhere the other kids got to go. "I've never been to Disney World. I'm sorry.

I didn't mean to say that—just thinking out loud."

"Then I'll take you to Disney World before the crazy of the season. Just you and me." He stopped talking, his eyes looked funny, then he cleared his throat. "Unless you want to go this week, but Disney is not fun when you're alone. I was just offering to keep you company is all."

"How about we wait until the season is over, after you win that ring like you keep saying you're going to. Don't they always ask what you're going to do now after you've won the Super Bowl? You can truthfully say you're going to Disney World. And it'll be cooler and less crowded and … I haven't forgotten that you're hiding something from me, Jaime."

"I promise, Pepper, I'm not hiding anything from you. It's just now that … the paparazzi are following me, trying to find dirt on me, and I don't want them dragging you into anything." He was lying. But why was he lying, she wondered.

"Or you don't want them thinking there's anything going on between me and you is more like it. I get it, Jaime. I'm not supermodel material, and you only date tall, busty blondes. I've seen the pictures."

"You have? I can explain."

"Explain what? That you date while you're out of town. What was her name last week while you were in LA? Ella Talbot, the actress from the new Bond movie? I get it.

Believe me I do. She is beautiful."

"That wasn't what it looked like, Cass, Ella and I were guests at the same party, and all that dating stuff is just lies. Heck, that was the only time we were even near each other all night. I swear." He sounded almost defensive.

"Jaime, you don't have to defend your life to me. I'm just your secretary. It's not like there's anything between us, is there?" She didn't dare look at him. She didn't want to see relief in his eyes. She sure as hell wasn't about to bring up the one night of unplanned sex that should never have happened. Nor would she mention that she really, really wished it would happen again.

"I don't know, Cass. I can't figure you out. Well, I'm going to have the codes changed on the front gate and the alarm updated this week. Just stay close to the house and pay attention to what's going on around you. If you notice anything out of the ordinary, call me, or the police. Okay? Promise me that much."

"Okay, Jaime. I promise." Somehow, she didn't think this had anything to do with the paparazzi. Something else was going on, but she knew Jaime Dalton well enough to know he'd already told her all she needed to know.

"That's good. I, uh, have to go. I need to call Mitch. That thing with the accountant is not going well." He took his package and disappeared in his office. Seconds later she heard the lock turn. He'd never locked her out before. Something was definitely going on. Something he didn't want her to know about.

Cass felt her skin crawl. Somehow, she had the strange feeling that she was being watched. It was just her imagination. Of course, Jaime's odd behavior had nothing whatsoever to do with giving her the heebie-jeebies. No, not at all. Now, thanks to him, she expected a camera-wielding psycho to jump out of the bushes in the backyard at any moment.

She did know one thing for certain, though. She really hated Jaime Dalton more and more every day.

* * * * *

She was late. Jaime paced his office, going to the front window to look out over the drive. On Sunday, she went to her book club and then for coffee with a couple of the women she met there. She was usually home long before dark. And the sun had definitely set over Miami, nearly an hour ago. Jaime checked his phone again. There was nothing, not even a text telling him the meeting had run long or that she was going to dinner.

He hated waiting and worrying, but he didn't call because he didn't want her knowing he was worried. He sure as hell didn't want her reading anything else into his worry. Cass wasn't easily misled. She'd almost had him cornered yesterday after the third package had arrived. He knew what he would find in this batch.

Mitch had hired someone to take care of it. Everything was going to be okay, as long as Cass was safe, and that was all that mattered. At least that's what he told himself. The simple fact was he didn't want anyone finding out what was in those packages. In the wrong hands … he shivered just thinking about it.

He heard the gate open before he saw the headlights. Right now, no one but Cass had the code to those gates, so it could only be her. He sure as hell didn't want her to catch him standing at the front window watching for her.

A few minutes later, she let herself in the front door, and he released the breath he hadn't realized he'd been holding. He shuffled papers around on his desk, pretending to look at contracts as she walked in, much like that first day back home. He looked up just as she dropped a couple of shopping bags in the chair nearest the door.

"Hey, you're home already?" She had a wistful smile on her face. Her eyes were sort of dreamy and soft. Had she met someone?

"How was book club?"

"It was nice." Her voice was sort of far away and gravelly. Either she'd been drinking or she had definitely met someone. "We talked about the book and stuff."

"Oh yeah? What are you reading? Is it good?" He leaned back in his chair just as she leaned against the doorframe. She looked nice tonight; her hair was down and a bit windblown from the breeze outside. He liked that she never gooped stuff in it. She wore a sleeveless fitted tuxedo top over a short pencil skirt the color of the ocean.

"The new one by Stella Lawson. It's pretty good, but I'm withholding judgment until I finish it. Though I doubt you would like it; it doesn't have any pictures. And the plot is a little more complicated than 'Run, Spot, run.'" That was much better. That was the Cass Pendleton he knew and tolerated. "Let me know when you guys do *Green Eggs and Ham*, will ya, and I am so there."

"It's probably too complicated for you, but I'll be sure to let you know when we start *Pat the Bunny*. What are you doing here this time of night anyway? I thought you'd be off celebrating your last night of freedom."

"Just tying up loose ends before tomorrow." He stuffed the contract into an envelope and put it in the slot to go out tomorrow. "Have you eaten?"

"Yeah, there's a new bistro near the bookstore; a group of us went over." There was that smile again. She really had met someone and was nursing a little crush. "I thought you'd be out, or I would have brought something back for you."

"I've eaten, but thanks for the afterthought."

She fluffed her hair almost nervously as he stared at her. Had she let him run his fingers through her hair? Was that why she looked tousled? Had he kissed her? Her lips looked red and a little puffy. How long had she been seeing him?

"Okay, well, I'm sure you have a million things to do before tomorrow, so I'll get out of your way." She turned to leave and something inside him snapped. How dare she sneak around with some guy behind his back? Was she just waiting for him to leave to have her new *friend* over for a little show and tell? Not in his house.

"Cass, why don't you come in and close the door." There was no need to close the door. They were alone, no one to walk in on them. But he wanted the door closed. It was his house, she was his … whatever the hell she was, and she needed to do as she was told.

"Okay, what's up, Jaime?" She looked puzzled, but she did as he requested and closed the door.

"Lock it and come here."

She stared at him as if he'd lost his fucking mind. Maybe he had. Maybe he was one step away from the funny farm, but if he was, then it was her fault for sending him there.

She swallowed hard, but she locked the door as if it was a perfectly normal request and he wasn't dangerously close to a psychotic break.

"What are you going to do to me?" She glanced around the room nervously but she walked across the room, stopping just to the left of his desk. "Where do you want me?"

"There is good. You look very nice tonight."

"Thank you."

"Are you wearing a bra?" He'd never seen her bras, he realized then.

"Sure, why do you ask?" Her eyes grew suddenly leery. She stood straighter, as if she were trying to decide if she should run or see where this was going. Trouble was he didn't know where this was going; all he knew was that he had a horrible urge to know what color her bra was.

"Show me. Unbutton your blouse."

"Have you lost your mind?" She rested her fingers over the top button before she thought to question his sanity, and as he watched, her nipples grew sharp against the fitted material.

"Most assuredly. But that's immaterial. The way I see it, Pepper, I've never once seen you in a bra, and I'd like to remedy that situation. So you have two options: run and lock yourself in your bedroom, or do as I ask and unbutton your blouse."

"You're a jerk. You do know that, don't you?" He noticed that she didn't turn and run, and that she fiddled with the little white button just above her breastbone as if thinking it over.

"Miss Pendleton, do as you are told, or I will be forced to punish you." Her eyes grew smoky, and as he watched, her nipples grew harder, her breathing rapid.

"I hate you," she said through gritted teeth, but that top button came free, followed by the second and so on, until she stood before him with her blouse gaping open and liquid fire in her eyes.

Damn, Pepper was hot when she was turned on. "Slide it down your arms. Slowly, Pepper. Yeah, that's nice."

The material cupping her breasts was white with little pink rosebuds, with an underwire that gave her incredible cleavage. Round, soft, honey-toned—did he mention soft? He licked his lips that had suddenly gone dry the second her shirt hit the floor.

"There, are you happy?"

"Mmm, baby, not by a long shot. Now the skirt. I want to see those pretty panties."

"Jaime, what's really going on here?" she

asked, but that didn't stop her from sliding the zipper down her hip and wiggling the skirt down her legs very slowly.

"Just think of it like this: you'll be sending me off to war a happy man."

"You're not a soldier. You're just a horn dog."

"And right now, babe, I'm horny for you. Step out of that skirt and come over here."

"I think this is about as close as I should get to you right now. At least until I know what your exact intentions are."

"Well, babe, remember in New York I asked you a question."

"Yeah, I remember." Her face grew pale; the liquid smoke left her eyes.

"I think I'm aiming to collect on that request."

"This is hardly public."

She did remember. "So you are spared that at least. Now, Pepper. I want to feel your mouth on me now, before I explode from thinking about it."

"So let me get this straight, you want a

blowjob so bad you tried to trick me into it."

"Well, when you put it that way, it sounds dirty. I really want to see your panties, and I want a blowjob. It's more of a win-win situation."

"Really? What's in it for me? From where I'm standing, the only person winning anything in this arrangement is you."

"I don't know, Pepper. I'm told I have very talented hands, and I'm also told I'm pretty good with my mouth too." He stuck his tongue out just to taunt her. "Your nipples are hard, Pepper."

"I know it; shut up. I can't think when you talk. Dammit, Jaime, this isn't funny—this, whatever the hell this is. I can't keep this up."

"I agree, Pepper, while you're standing there doing nothing I want you to cup your breasts." She just stared at him as if he'd lost his mind, but she did as he asked. "That's it, baby, lift them high. Oh yeah, Pepper, that looks nice."

"I still hate you."

"Hate me all you want, but you lust after me,

and that's all I need to know. Now, Pepper, I want you to take your nipples between your fingers and stroke them. Imagine it's my mouth. Would you like my mouth on your nipples, Pepper?"

"Yes." Her eyes rolled to the back of her head as she moaned.

"Tell me what you want me to do to your nipples, Pepper, suck them, bite them.

Ohh, look at how hard they are, Pepper. You are making me hard. Come sit in my lap so I can see."

"Jaime, don't make me do this." She walked toward him, teetering on another pair of those wedge-heeled sandal things that tied around her ankles.

"I like those shoes; what do you call them?"

"They are espadrilles. Do you want me to take them off?"

"Hell no, give me one." She lifted her foot, balancing in front of him on the other.

She shivered when he stroked her leg, placing

her foot on the chair beside his thigh.

"That's pretty, Pepper. I like pink panties on you. And what's that I see—a wet spot between your legs? Pepper, you ought to be ashamed of yourself. Standing there showing me your little wet pussy like that. Say you're sorry."

"Jaime." Her protest came out as a throaty sigh.

"Say you're sorry, Pepper." Goddamn, the spot grew darker as he watched.

"I'm sorry, Jaime. Are you going to spank me?"

"Oh God, woman, don't say such things. You just made my cock jerk in my pants."

"I'm sorry my pussy is wet, Jaime. It wants your cock inside it."

"Pepper, stop that, it's naughty. Are you a naughty, naughty girl? I like naughty girls, did you know that?"

"I suspected as much."

"How naughty are you, Pepper? Naughty

enough to slide your fingers inside your panties and pet your pretty little pussy for me?"

"Jaime…"

"Lord Ironman, to you, or Master. We've had that discussion before. Now pet your pussy for me, Pepper."

God help him, he thought she'd hit her limit for one night, the look she gave him was indescribable, bordering on outright hate. As he watched, she eased her right hand down her belly and beneath the pink lace. She rolled her eyes again, her breath catching on a sigh.

"Stroke your clit, Pepper. No, don't go deeper, just your clit, baby." He ran his hand up and down her leg in encouragement. She looked out at him between slitted eyes, blue fire burning behind her lashes as she pleasured herself. "Make yourself come for me, baby. Oh, that is so sweet, baby. Does that feel good? Does your hand feel good, Pepper?

Come for me, baby." He leaned forward and

kissed the inside of her thigh. The contact set her leg to quivering.

"That feels so good, Jaime." She was so close to losing control. Her breath became ragged; her chest rose and fell in time to the rhythm she set with her finger. "So good, I can't … I'm so … that feels so good."

He couldn't take it any longer. He snagged the crotch of her panties and pulled the material to the side so he could see her play with her clit. "Slide your finger inside, Pepper. Oh yeah, baby, just like that."

The sound that came from her throat was more of a purr than a moan or a groan. She hitched her hip forward to slide deeper, and Jaime found himself trying to stop the moan that was trapped inside his chest. "How does that feel, baby?" But Pepper was long past answering. She leaned her head back, her mouth slack, her eyes closed. "Jaime," she said in a long whispered keening way that sent electricity shooting to the tips of his toes and back to his cock.

"Yeah, baby, that is so nice, Pepper, so nice."

"I'm coming, Jaime."

"I know, baby. Come for me, Pepper. That's my girl." She flung her head wildly, her skin glowing red as heat rushed through her. Her thighs began to tremble, and just when he thought she would lose her balance, she screamed out his name, followed by a string of obscenities.

* * * * *

Aware that she stood straddling Jaime Dalton's lap with her finger deep inside her body, Cass drew in a shocked breath. How in the hell had she let him goad her into this, she wondered. Why did she lose all sense when it came to him?

"That was beautiful, Pepper," his voice was deep, breathy, his hand on her leg hot, as he stroked her. *Oh yeah, that's how.* Jaime could seduce the panties off a mannequin if he wanted to. "You're creamy, did you know."

She hastily pulled her hand from inside her

panties, intending to escape with what was left of her dignity intact, but Jaime had other ideas. He caught her hand in his and drew her fingers into his mouth. And just like that, all of her resolve fled right out of the room, leaving her behind, weak and defenseless, when it came to him.

"You taste so sweet, did you know that?"

"No." Oh God, what was she doing?

He suckled her fingers, drawing on them as if his very life depended on the sustenance he found there. The pressure coursed up her arm, causing tiny bolts of electricity to shoot to that very spot her finger had just vacated.

"Then we should do something about that," he said, but before she could figure out what he meant, he tugged her panties down her legs. She teetered on low heels while he dragged the fabric off and tossed them on the floor. "Come here." He pulled her into his lap, settling a knee on each side of his thighs, and before she could catch her breath, he cupped her pussy with one of his large hands, sinking a long slender finger deep inside her. "Oh yeah, Pepper, such a sweet, slick little pussy, already creamy and ready for seconds."

She wanted to argue with him, but he knew just where to stroke her, and somehow the only thing that came out of her mouth was pleas for more and harder. "Please, Jaime, let me taste you."

"Too late for that, darlin'; you had your chance earlier, but your mouth got in the way."

"I'm sorry, Jaime, I want to taste you. Please." She held onto his shoulders, fighting this incredible need she had to gyrate on his finger. He slipped a second inside her, and she cried out. "Please."

"Please what, Pepper? What do you want to do to me? Tell me, Pepper, do you want to suck my cock?"

"Yes." Oh, God, his fingers felt so good, going deeper than she could reach. He touched that spot that made her crazy.

"Then say it, make me believe it."

"I want to suck your cock. Please, Jaime, I want to taste you. Let me suck you."

"Do you know what I really want right now, Pepper?"

"No, Jaime, tell me," she hissed the words as he drove into her, pushing her past all sanity. "Tell me. I'm going to come, Jaime. Do that again."

"I want you to open your pretty mouth for me, Pepper." He drove into her again, his fiery gaze locked on hers the only thing that kept her from exploding right then. "I want to see your face when you taste your cream, Pepper." Her body throbbed from the loss of his hot fingers, but she did as he told her and opened her mouth. "Suck my fingers, Pepper. Suck your cream from my fingers." She did, God help her, she did. She tasted tangy and a little sweet, sparks shot through his golden eyes as he watched her pull his fingers into her mouth and latch on, suckling as if her life depended on it. His stifled moan of pleasure made her feel powerful.

"God damn, Pepper, you have a nasty mouth." He swiveled the chair, and she heard him open a desk drawer. "Open my pants, baby. It's time to take this game to the next level."

She obeyed. God damn him to hell, but she couldn't help herself. The button on his jeans gave her a little trouble, but the zipper slid down easily, and his silky cock was hot and hard in her hands before he could free his fingers from her mouth. "My turn."

"Next time, baby. Right now, if you put that nasty little mouth of yours on me this will be all over." Disappointed, she watched as he covered himself with a condom. "We don't need this anymore." She felt his hands on her back, the straps of her bra slid down her arms, leaving her naked and at the mercy of his quick hands.

"I love your tits, Pepper. Christ, I could come just looking at you." He pulled her against his body, the buttons of his shirt rough against her belly. "Lift them up for me, just like you did a little while ago. Higher. Oh yeah, right there is perfect." She held her breasts to his mouth, offering him her soul. In return, he wrapped his arms around her and cupped her ass cheeks.

Pulling her closer, he latched on to one nipple, suckling it hard and deep before moving on to the other. Then, as if she weighed nothing, he lifted her just high enough to plunge deep inside her.

Chapter Thirteen

The house was quiet. Too quiet. Cass lay in bed until nearly noon listening to the quiet. She knew she was alone. She'd known, almost to the moment, when Jaime left, as if she were somehow attuned to him. The thought demolished her.

She had no reason to believe there could ever be a connection between Jaime and herself. He was simply what he claimed to be, horny, and she was the only thing with a vagina available.

He'd used her, abused her, and used her some more during the course of the evening.

And she was just so happy to be there she did every vile, disturbing thing he asked of her.

If he were to walk into her room right that very second, command her to strip naked, and dance the hula, she would.

That thought sent her back beneath the covers. Covers that reeked of Jaime's cologne and sex. Why hadn't he carried her to his room? Why did it have to be hers?

So he could leave when he was finished with her.

Such a no-brainer, that one was.

And finish with her, he did. Sometime around dawn, she finally gave him what he wanted in the first place. Then he was gone. An hour later, when she heard the front gates open and close, she knew he was gone.

In a fit of misery, she jumped from the bed, ripping the linen off and throwing it in a pile on the floor. She hated the damned stuff anyway. It looked like the ocean had exploded with all the blues and greens. What was with the purple sheets anyway?

After a shower, she found herself pacing the house looking for something to do.

Breakfast held no appeal for her. Neither did

the book club book. She ran the washer, threw in the ugly purple sheets and the comforter, and washed the dishes left over from the night before. Then, she poked around the garden looking for weeds, swept the floors, hauled out the vacuum, and cleaned the perfectly pristine brand-new carpeting. Though when she got to the office, she grabbed the knob and slammed it closed. She just could not face that room today.

At two she went down to the school, read stories to the kids, helped the summer school kids with their homework, and listened to them ask about Jaime and if he'd bring them little team logo footballs the next time he came. She promised he would, even if she had to call up the home office and order them herself.

At five, she called her mom to see how she was enjoying her trip to Vegas. Her mom was busy having a good time.

She drove by the bistro. David Cooper's car was parked outside. She thought about stopping.

She thought about the conversation they'd had the night before about practically everything and that he asked if he could call her. Then, she thought about the things she let Jaime Dalton do to her right after she'd left David.

She realized as she sat and watched for him to leave the restaurant, there was no reason to lead David on. This thing with Jaime did not need any more complication, and David would be nothing but a complication.

She drove on, finding herself at Bed Bath and Beyond. Thoughts of the atrocious bedding in her room running through her mind, she decided that she would make the guest suite into her own domain starting today with the purging of the aquarium bedding.

An hour later, she emerged with enough linen to stock a small store. Not to mention all of the accessories to match. New curtains, bath mat, throw pillows. It was a step in the right direction. Even if that direction meant being Jaime Dalton's sometime plaything, then so be it.

She ate a late meal alone, watched television alone, and roamed the house restlessly.

It was too quiet.

At midnight, she crawled between the freshly laundered stark-white Egyptian cotton sheets and felt at home for the first time in months. She sighed when the gate lumbered open and then closed. She stretched beneath the covers completely relaxed now that she knew he was home.

His heavy tread on the stairs told her he was tired, he would probably get a few hours sleep before he had to leave again. She waited for him to make the turn to his side of the house. Instead, her door opened quietly on its hinges, and his warm body slid into bed beside her. He pulled her beneath him and with lightning-fast hands that swept her breath away; he stripped her to her skin. Before she could say hello, he was deep inside her.

"I didn't have time to pick up condoms; are you on birth control?" was all he said as he moved inside her, robbing her of breath. She shook her head. He groaned. "It's all right, I'll pull out."

The next morning he placed a kiss on her shoulder. She opened her eyes wide enough to see his body in the pale light of dawn; the bruises that covered his skin made her cringe.

"Have a good day," she told him when he kissed her cheek. Then he was gone and something fluttered in her stomach. A small electric thrill of something forbidden and almost sweet.

Cass went back to sleep after the gate closed behind him. She would have to wash the sheets again. Somehow, that was all right.

* * * * *

All week long Jaime counted the minutes until quitting time. Tired, bruised, and completely wrung out, he dragged home every night instead of falling into the bunk reserved for him in the dorm. Always his intention was to check on her, make sure she was fine, and fall into his own bed. However, those intentions always fell to the wayside the second he saw her. Night after night, he went to her room, and each morning he awakened in her bed.

During the day, he worked harder than he ever remembered working before. There was a calmness in his soul that he didn't recognize. He threw longer and seemed to breeze through workouts. Of course that didn't mean the hits were any easier to take, especially the hits without pads.

There was an energetic atmosphere that week. Almost fun. Everyone from the towel boys on up fell into step, working as if they were one machine. This was the year. He knew it, the year he would take his team to the big game, the year they would bring home the trophy. Everything was falling into place. Saturday would be the test. The first preseason game, Saturday in Minnesota, they would show the world that this was their year.

Thursday evening he drove home earlier than usual, pulling into the garage just before nine instead of nearly midnight.

He expected to find her somewhere in the house, trying to keep herself busy, but as he passed room after darkened room unease assailed him. Upstairs her door was open.

The lamp on her vanity was on, but she wasn't there.

Her car was out front, her clothes still hung in her closet, and her purse lay on her bed. There was a heavy scent of vanilla in the air, he followed it to the bathroom, and without thinking, he opened the door.

She stood under the rainfall shower, her back to him, rinsing shampoo from her hair.

He didn't make a noise, he didn't even dare breath for fear that this was all a mirage and he was in fact lying in the middle of the football field dying of sunstroke. But almost as if she sensed his presence, she turned, her eyes meeting his, a smile of welcome on her lips.

He didn't need any more encouragement than that. In seconds flat, he left his clothes lying on the floor and stepped into the shower with her. She stepped into his arms, her body, warm and wet, felt so nice against his.

"How was your day?" She gingerly touched the bruise that covered his left hip.

"Rough." He took the bottle of body wash from her, and using nothing but his hands, he bathed every tender nook and cranny of her sensitive body, lingering on those spots that elicited the greatest reaction. When he couldn't control himself another second, he lifted her against the wall, and in no time he was home, where he belonged.

*****

"I didn't know the ceiling in here was blue." She heard him say, his voice was thick from sleep. His voice rumbled in his chest just below her ear. "It's always been like that," she answered after a few moments of trying to clear the cotton from her brain. "Why are you still here?"

"I like the blue; makes the room feel sort of, I don't know, serene. I like these sheets too. Soft." He laid his arm over her shoulders and just held her, his voice still sleepy, his body so warm she could stay next to him the rest of the day. "It's raining outside."

"I know. I hear it. Still doesn't answer my question."

"We leave for Minnesota tonight, so no practice. Do you want to go to Minnesota? I can arrange things if you do."

"What's in Minnesota?" She honestly could not remember what his schedule this week entailed. She left this one up to him.

"First preseason game against the Vikes. So do you want to go? I hear it's already cooling down up there, so you might need to take something warm."

"It's just the first week of August. I don't have anything warm."

"Baby, you probably need to start looking for some winter clothes. Even if you don't go this weekend, I am going to drag you to a game or two once the regular season opens.

Probably to that Packers game. That's an idea, why don't I get your mom tickets to the Packers game, and I'll fly you both up. Think she'd like that?"

"Probably. Jaime?"

"Yeah?"

"Shut up and go back to sleep."

"What if I have other things on my mind?" He took her hand in his and laid it over a certain part of his anatomy that was indeed very much awake.

"Then you need to go handle it yourself or call one of your bimbos, because I am worn out." She smiled against his chest when he gasped after she closed her fingers around his arousal and squeezed. "At least give me another hour of sleep." Before she finished speaking, she found herself lying on her back with a very awake man between her legs, his erection hot and heavy against her pelvis. "Jaime!"

"Pepper!" He eased down her body just a fraction, a look of intense concentration on his face as he eased inside her. "Sleep can wait."

"Yes, it can." She hooked her legs over his hips and held on for the ride. It wasn't long before she was spiraling into the stratosphere. Jaime sank his teeth into her collarbone, his body growing tight, his movements quick and precise. "Jaime! No condom. Pull out." She crashed down to earth, her body screaming for her mind to shut up.

He didn't hesitate, sliding from her body without releasing her shoulder until his orgasm passed.

His almost angelic face hovered over hers, his lips grazed hers, his golden eyes shimmered as he held her beneath him. Something was different about him. Something that she couldn't quite put her finger on. "You've cut all of your hair off."

"Why is it you just now noticed that?" He smiled down at her, while sliding his body against hers, as he nibbled her chin and worked his way lower. "It was that, or borrow one of your hair thingies to keep it out of my eyes."

"What are you doing?" She ran her hands over his very close-cropped head as he nibbled his way lower, pausing at her chest long enough to start her gasping for air.

"Jaime?"

"You didn't finish. I'm taking care of that."

"How do you know I didn't finish?" He didn't answer. Instead, he lifted her legs and settled between them, dipping his golden head to taste her. When she finally went over, he crawled up the length of her body and laid his head on her shoulder.

"Because you come with your whole body, Pepper. You can't hide that from me." He pressed his lips to hers, the devil in his amber eyes smiling down at her as he pulled the covers up. "Now be quiet and go back to sleep."

"Jaime?" She didn't know what she wanted to say, but it didn't matter. He was asleep, lying draped across her body, his breathing slow and even as if he'd never been awake in the first place. "Damn it, Jaime, what are you doing to me?" Of course, he didn't answer, and now she was wide-awake with nothing better to do than hold him while he slept, because whether she liked it or not, tomorrow he would be gone.

Chapter Fourteen

The rain didn't let up until after noon. Sometime before that, Cass managed to extricate herself from beneath the behemoth who, for some reason, preferred sleeping on her instead of beside her. Showered and dressed in a pair of shorts and one of Jaime's football T-shirts she'd stolen from the laundry, she went downstairs to start breakfast.

She'd just flipped the last pancake onto a platter when she heard the gate buzzer.

Jaime hadn't told her to expect anyone, and she hadn't ordered anything. Curious she went to the box near the front door just as Jaime appeared on the landing.

"Who is it?"

"I don't know yet," she shushed him and

pressed the intercom. "Can I help you?"

"Dade County Police department. Is this the residence of Jamison Dalton?" The face on the screen was slightly distorted from the rain. He could be anyone.

Jaime looked somewhat pale when she looked up at him to see what he wanted her to do. He just shrugged.

"Show me your badge, please."

A shiny metal object flashed in front of the camera.

"It looks real. Did you do something I need to know about?"

"Aw, Pepper is willing to alibi for me. That is so sweet." His grin was infectious.

"Let's see what he wants."

"You might want to put on some clothes. And stop dripping on the floor. I just mopped up there yesterday."

A few moments later, she greeted one of Miami's finest with a smile and offered him something to drink. He simply stood looking at her with surprise in his eyes.

"What's your name?" He flipped open a notebook.

"Cassandra Pendleton, and if you don't mind turning that question back on yourself, I'd feel a little less defensive right about now."

"Detective Ryan. Do you live here?" He really was short and to the point.

"Live here and work here, among other things. And this is relevant because?"

"Is Jamison Dalton at home? We have some questions for him."

"He just stepped out of the shower. He should be down…"

"I'm here. Pepper, is there something burning in the kitchen?" The acrid scent of burning meat sent her scurrying to the back of the house. The last thing she saw was the detective's curious eyes as he shifted from her to Jaime and then back to her.

"What can I do for one of Miami's finest, this fine afternoon?" Was the last thing she heard Jaime say before she found the kitchen filled with smoke and the bacon a charred mess in the pan.

"Shit." She carried the pan out onto the patio and left it to cool. She left the doors open and turned on the fans to clear the air. Quickly making sure everything was turned off, she walked back to the front of the house. The heat in Jaime's voice stopped her cold, and she leaned against the wall to listen.

"Where did you get that picture?"

"Is the woman in this picture the same woman I just met?"

"I don't see how that's any of your business?"

"Just answer the question, Mr. Dalton. Is this woman Cassandra Pendleton?" Her skin crawling as if something vile had slithered over her, Cass stepped quietly into the room to find Jaime sitting behind his desk his face a mask of rage.

"May I see the photo?" She held her hand out,

and the detective looked between them before he handed it to her.

"Cass, you probably shouldn't..."

Her stomach lurched. She had to reach for the desk to steady herself. "Where did this come from?"

"Is that you, Miss Pendleton?" The detective's voice took on a different tone. She merely nodded. There were no words.

"I see. And was that consensual?" He nodded toward the photo.

"Yes." She looked again her heart jumped into her throat. The clear image of her and Jaime on the patio that first day, her arms bound behind her, her eyes covered, her body clearly outlined beneath her cotton gown grew worse as she stared at it. "How ... where ... who? Oh God."

"Why are you really here, detective?" His face grew hard. Angry fire seemed to beam from behind his eyes. He bristled with power and rage as he paced the room.

Cass searched for a chair to collapse into, the photo shaking in her hand until the detective reached over and retrieved it.

"This was mailed to me with a tip that you were holding a young woman here against her will. No return address and no signature. I was obligated to check."

"How could someone have pictures of us on the patio? I don't understand. The property is completely enclosed. Whoever it was would have to have been standing—"

"Somewhere in the bushes on the other side of the pool. Yeah, I know, I've gone over that entire area. I've changed all of the locks and security codes. I just don't know." He was like a caged animal, trapped and ready to gnaw himself free.

"You knew about this picture? Why didn't you tell me?" She lashed out and then she could see things perfectly clear, things made sense now. "Those FedEx packages. There are more pictures, aren't there? Jaime, are there more pictures of us?"

"Pepper…"

"Don't Pepper me. Jaime, are there more pictures of us from that day?"

"That day, and in New York, others of us around town together."

"May I see them?" The detective asked in the charged silence.

"Do you know who took them? What do they want?"

"Money, they want money, or they are going to sell them to some magazine. I'll look like a pervert and probably be fined and suspended for conduct unbecoming — stuff like that. They want to hurt me." He opened a locked cabinet that held a safe she was unaware of, pulled out three envelopes, and handed them over to detective Ryan.

"Why didn't you call the police?" he said after looking though the images, his eyes going to her several times.

"I had my people looking into it. My lawyer

has a private detective watching the house, and we've hired a private security firm to keep tabs on Cass, just in case."

"But you didn't pay them?" Ryan closed the last envelope and reluctantly offered them to her. Her heart slamming in her chest she took them and regretted every single second of it, but she had to know.

Images of her naked in Jaime's lap that stormy afternoon. Of them waiting for the elevator in New York, her arms already bound behind her, her scarf over her eyes. The third held images of her standing on the beach, the bruise on her shoulder from Jaime's teeth clearly visible. Of her at the grocery store and other places in town, and standing in the kitchen or sitting in the garage. "There's another envelope. It arrived by regular mail yesterday. I put it in the file over there."

Nausea gripped her belly, fear her heart as she waited for Jaime to fish through the mail slot and pull out the priority envelope. His face grew ashen as he flipped through the pages.

"These are from Sunday night. Through the window." He nodded his head toward the front of the house. "And Monday. Son of a bitch can see into your room."

"What do we do now?" She didn't want to see these. Shaking her head when the detective held one out to her.

"Who is this?" he asked her pointing to the tall, slim, dark-haired man she was standing with outside the bookstore. "There are several of you with him."

"David Cooper. I met him at book club week before last."

"And you had dinner with him Sunday." There was accusation in his eyes.

"And then I came home and had sex with you. I haven't seen him since. Christ, Jaime, now is not the time to explore this … this dysfunctional thing we have between us."

"There isn't a letter this time." The detective

sighed. "Looks like someone is stalking the two of you. Someone angry with you, Mr. Dalton, who wants to hurt you. If you want my opinion, Miss Pendleton may be in danger."

"I know." Jaime leaned his head against the window frame. She could see his eyes scanning the property. "I just don't know how they are getting onto my property. Like Cass said, it's completely surrounded by a high brick wall, and the only two gates are secure."

"They'll go to the media next. You know that, don't you?"

"Yes." His voice rumbled from his chest. His body grew tense with anger and impotence.

"Cass. Go pack. I'm not leaving you here alone this weekend. You're coming to Minnesota with me. You'll be safe from whoever is climbing the fucking trees to watch you sleep."

"No." Panic tightened her chest. "I'm going to go home for a few days. I don't want to be with strangers when this hits the internet."

"Will you come back?"

"I don't know." Cass couldn't think straight. Fear had a way of robbing her of rational thought. "Maybe this is for the best, Jaime. Things are too confused right now.   Maybe it would be better if I didn't."

"I'll … don't worry, baby, I'll make the arrangements. Go pack your bags." She could have sworn he was going to say something else, or start an argument or otherwise talk her out of staying away. He seemed defeated when he sat in his desk chair across from the detective. His shoulders slumped, but the fear she saw in his eyes told her he would respect her decision.

* * * * *

After Detective Ryan left, Jaime sat puzzled for a while. The questions the detective asked after Cass had left the room only served to open up a treasure trove of unanswered questions. Who exactly had he pissed off enough for this kind of harassment? Who exactly? He had no effin' idea.

The paparazzi in general, but they usually sold their ill-gotten gains to the highest bidder. Blackmail and then sending damning photos to the cops didn't seem to be their MO. Cam at the Cameron Agency? Possibly, but the first photos predated his knowledge of the embezzlement, so Cam wouldn't have been looking for his head at that time. A rival football team out to throw him off his game? Always possible, but highly unlikely.

If he had any enemies, they were on the field and nothing that would go beyond the field.

Questions arose about his recent trip to France and the reason for his early return back to the states. Jaime simply refused to believe that had anything to do with this. No, he'd left France with no worries.

He picked up the phone and called his lawyer to fill him in. Mitch seemed relieved that the police were now involved. Jaime wasn't so sure.

Monday he had to go to the precinct and file

an official complaint, but Detective Ryan seemed genuinely interested in doing what he could to help him find who was doing this. Jaime suspected it was more for Cass's sake than his since he now knew her dirty little secret. And what she looked like naked. Somehow, that didn't sit well with Jaime.

After he called the airline, booked Cass to Birmingham, and then scheduled a rental car to get her the rest of way home, he went upstairs to check on her.

"When do you leave?" She saw him out of the corner of her eye as she moved from closet to dresser to bed folding garments and basically freaking out.

"Later tonight. I've got you a flight leaving in two hours. Are you sure you want to go?" He asked hoping she would change her mind and come with him. He had a terrible feeling that if she went home he would never see her again. Right now, he didn't know how he felt about that.

"I'm sure. Hand me those shoes, will you?" She didn't look at him for too long; her eyes met his and then looked hastily away. Her hands shook when he touched her.

This was all his fault. He shouldn't have kept this from her. Hell, he should have stayed away from her in the first place, and then there wouldn't be any X-rated pictures floating around out there. Then he noticed what she was wearing and suddenly everything was fine.

"Hey, Pepper. I like your shirt." He grinned at her, his eyes going pointedly to the logo displayed prominently over her breasts that read *Property number 4 Miami Football*.

She'd borrowed one of his team shirts with his name on the back. No wonder that detective kept looking at her funny. "I believe that falls under the heading of ironic. What do you think?"

He left her standing there with her mouth open. He knew the scathing retort would probably be more like a shoe flung at his head. Retreat for now was the best course. This would pass, and Cass would have a nice week with her mom, and everything would be all right. This was his year. Everything was going according to plan.

Mercy Celeste

Chapter Fifteen

"Things obviously aren't going according to plan," Cass's mom Gloria said when Jaime threw his helmet across the field. Rage reflected in his face, eyes — hell, in his whole body. He got into a team member's face screaming what looked like obscenities and threats. That same team member had just dropped a perfectly thrown ball in the end zone. "Looks like that's the game, sweetie. Jaime had a bad day. The team had a bad day. It's just the first preseason game, no worries."

"He looks so angry out there." Cass couldn't take her eyes off him, the black smudges on his cheeks brought out the fire in his amber eyes. Sweat coated his body, dripping into his eyes. Minnesota was in the middle of a freak heat wave apparently. He was like an animal, predatory, calculating, and ruthless. The way he moved simply amazed her; at one point he jumped over a guy running headlong at him before he threw the ball. "So…"

"Masculine. The boy grew into one fine specimen of a man, Cass. Tight in all the right places, if you know what I mean."

"Mom! I am shocked. Shocked." And embarrassed to know just how tight some of those places really were, but she wasn't about to tell her mother that.

"So I'm just a mangy old cougar. Live with it. While we're talking about tight, why are you really home? Don't lie to me, Cassandra. What's going on between you and Jaime?"

"Nothing. I can't come home for a vacation?"

"Cut the crap. You're sleeping with him. I can see that much, and that alone is probably enough to send you running for the hills."

"I am not sleeping with Jaime Dalton." She hesitated too long before protesting. Her mother raised her eyebrows in that frustrating look she always wore when Cass was trying to talk her way out of whatever trouble she was in growing up.

"Bullshit, you have that well-laid glow about you. About time, too. I knew if the two of you could stop bickering long enough you'd figure it out."

"I am not sleeping with him. And what makes you think we've done anything but bicker and fight. Jaime still is and has always been a huge prick."

"Yeah, and I bet he has one too. Just look at that boy's hands."

"Mother! We are not having this conversation. Not today, not ever."

"Okay, have it your way, Cass. Hide out as long as you need. Just remember you dragged in here after midnight last night with no warning. So don't expect me to hang around to be your shoulder. I've got plans." Gloria patted her on her leg and left her sitting in the living room watching the tail end of her very first football game. Miami had just lost twenty-four to ten.

She sat through the post-game interviews, where a sweaty, agitated Jaime evaded questions about his performance, praised his teammates and the other team, and promised a better showing the following week back home in Miami. She saw past the forced bravado into his eyes. She knew that look well. He was on edge, stressed to the point of breaking. Guilt washed over her. Maybe if she had gone with him…

No, this was not her fault. Whoever was stalking him was solely at fault. If that day on the patio had never happened or that night in New York, she couldn't help rationalizing, there would be no dirty pictures. She would still be in Miami waiting for him to come home instead of hiding out in her mother's living room.

"Shit." She switched off the TV, angry with herself for letting any of this happen in the first place. Sex with Jaime was her mistake. One she wouldn't make again, if she went back.

After dinner, her mom called out for her not to wait up and left Cass with the dishes.

She had the Cooking Channel on watching Giada cook something that looked sinfully simple but she knew it wouldn't be, when her phone rang. She knew that ring, not that she had a special tone set just for him, but somehow it just rang differently when he called. She let it ring a few times as she wiped the table and put away the casserole pan before she answered it.

"Tough game." She said even though she promised herself to stay neutral and keep it short and sweet.

"It shouldn't have been. I was off, and it affected the guys. Should have been an easy win." Just the sound of his voice made her tingle all over. "So how is your mom? Tell her hey for me."

"She's out somewhere having a life." She settled onto the sectional sofa and turned the TV to mute. "Where are you?"

"In a hotel, waiting for dinner, thinking about going down to the hot tub. I've got bruises on top of bruises." She heard him grunt as he moved around on his end.

"I feel for you. I really do. Okay, I don't. You do know those bruises are avoidable, right?"

"Sure, I didn't have to play ball. I could have gone on to medical school or law school. Don't snort, Miss Summa Cum Laude. I do have a brain in my head."

"Not for too much longer if you keep getting knocked upside it like that." She cringed, thinking about the headlong charges he'd endured during the course of the game. Many of which she'd covered her eyes during out of fear.

"True, that. Hey, what are you doing right now?"

"Sitting on the couch, talking to you and watching TV on mute."

"Yeah, anything good on?"

"Not particularly. It's a Saturday night,

nothing but reruns of reruns. Ooh look, a Scooby Doo movie that ought to be right up your alley."

"Mmm, Daphne. She was hot."

"Daphne was a bimbo. Velma, now there was a woman. She rocked that orange miniskirt and had brains."

"Yeah, but Velma was blind as a bat. She did have some major tits under that sweater, so I could see it. You know, I always wondered what Fred and Daphne did when they split off from the group."

"Really? I always wondered what Fred, Daphne, *and* Velma did when they sent Shag and Scooby off on their own."

He laughed; the sound low and sensuous vibrated over the line. "That's because you are a bit on the twisted side. I like that about you, Pepper."

"And you're not the slightest bit twisted? Come on. You let guys beat you up for a living. That, Mr. Dalton, is beyond twisted. It's messed up."

"Hey, got to pay for the lifestyle somehow."

"What lifestyle? You pretend to have a lifestyle but, from what I can tell, Mr. Dalton, you are tight-fisted with your money. Yeah, you have a nice house almost on the water, and a couple of cars, one of which is a station wagon, I might add."

"Hey, you're the one who picked out that wagon. I was thinking more of a second sports car. Besides, I keep you in designer duds, don't I?" He didn't sound the least bit offended.

"If by designer, you mean that discount stuff I picked up at Target and Kohl's, then okay, sure. You do know most of that furniture I bought for your house came from Rooms To Go and IKEA, right? Hardly high end."

"So, it looks nice. Did I tell you, that I like the old stuff you redid better than the fancy furniture the designer bought three years ago?"

"No, you didn't tell me. Even the console I

painted turquoise?"

"It looks nice in the dining room. When are we going to get a table in there anyway?"

"Why? You never have people over, and you eat standing over the sink."

"I can think of a couple of things to do on that table other than eat."

"I am not having that conversation with you. Not tonight. So, when will you be home?"

"Tomorrow afternoon sometime." He sounded disappointed, but she wasn't ready to go down that path, innocent or not. "When are you planning on coming home?"

"I just got here, jeez, I haven't even unpacked yet."

"That just makes coming home easier."

"Yeah, well, I think I'm going to hang out here a while. Visit some friends, stuff like that."

"Okay, sounds like a good plan. Go say hi to my mom, will you?"

"Sure. Hey, Jaime?"

"Yeah?"

"You sound tired. Did you sleep last night?"

"Not really, that's why I played like shit today, I guess. Hey, Pepper?"

"Yeah?"

He hesitated, his breath heavy on the line. "Food is here, I'm going to go eat now."

"Yeah, and get some sleep."

"You, too. Okay, so yeah, um, good night."

"You, too, Jaime." Then he was gone. Deflated and oddly agitated, she thought he was about to say something else. Like, maybe, that he missed her.

But why would Jaime Dalton miss her? She turned off the television. Her own sleepless night finally caught up with her and went to bed.

During the day, Cass was fine. She put on her happiest face and went out with old friends. She even managed to drop by and visit with Jaime's mom, who was incredibly happy to see her. At night, she couldn't stop the demons from settling in to roost.

Most of her friends were settled in one way or another — marriage or career. Heck, two of the girls she went to high school with were not only married and teaching at the same school she'd been laid off from, they were expecting babies now as well.

Cass was far from settled. If she hadn't gotten off course and wasted two years in Nashville, if she'd chosen a different major, if she hadn't run out of money before she finished her doctorate. Too many ifs swirled in her head. That left her agitated and unsatisfied.

During the day, she pretended she wasn't scared to death. She checked the internet gossip sites daily. She knew she was waiting for a reason not to go back. Day after day, there was nothing. Not one single mention of Jaime's name, except by football analysts who raked him across the coals for his performance the previous weekend. Clips of him working hard in the Miami sun, dressed in shorts, T-shirt, and helmet. Sometimes the shirt was totally missing, sometimes the helmet. She particularly loved that one shot of him wearing just a pair of sweaty running shorts, his skin golden and glistening with sweat as he leaned his hands on his knees trying to catch his breath.

Every night she waited for his call. Every night she sat in the living room alone, wondering why he never said he missed her.

On Saturday, Cass roamed the house, bored out of her mind. The sun was shining outside, the world was spinning around, yet she turned down three invitations for shopping, spa, or just hanging out at a friend's pool to stay home and be irritated and edgy.

She paced the house, which didn't take long. Two bedrooms, two baths connected to a living-dining-kitchen combo with a large back porch and a garage. Hardly large enough for just her mom, yet she'd grown up in this house and the walls suddenly seemed to want to reach out and suffocate her. Her room was tiny, the wallpaper faded and juvenile.

This wasn't home anymore.

To take her mind off her plight she found herself in the living room, remote in hand.

She tuned to the football channel just in time for the start of the pregame. Jaime in shoulder pads stood on the sidelines wearing a baseball cap. He looked rested and relaxed. For some reason, she felt the tension ease from her body as she watched him smile and goof off with the other guys. Now this was the Jaime she knew and…

The phone rang, and thinking it was her mom calling to check in, she answered without looking at the screen. She could see Jaime holding a phone to his ear take a seat on a bench, but even then she didn't think much of it until he spoke in that deep rumble that was his voice. Just like that, her stomach did this wild dance that sent warmth trailing to every square inch of her body.

"Hey, Pepper. What are you doing?"

"Aren't you supposed to be working?" She saw his lips hitch into a grin. "Stop grinning like that. People might think you're mad."

"How do you know I'm smiling?" He looked up his eyes staring directly into the camera. "Am I on TV?"

"Yeah, pretty boy. I'm sitting here watching you goof off. The announcers are wondering who you're talking to that makes you smile like that. Cut it out, it's embarrassing."

He laughed and raised his arm in the air and waved as he shouted, "Hi, Mom!"

"I'm not your mom, dufus. So why are you calling me. Aren't you supposed to be on the field doing footbally stuff?'

"I've got a little time. I thought I'd check in and see what you're up to. Say 'hi' to your mom." The camera panned away from him to cover the rest of his team who all seemed to be milling around the sidelines. The announcers, though, were still talking about Jaime's shout-out to his mom.

"She went with the Red Hats over to Tunica early this morning. I think my mom has developed a gambling problem since her trip to Vegas."

"Yeah, so you're alone, then?"

"No, smartass. I'm sitting with the pool boy. We're getting ready to go skinny-dipping."

"Lucky pool boy. Does he know you like to be tied up?"

"Jaime, don't start that."

"Pepper, I love when you get all defensive like that. Makes me think of bad things to do to you."

"I'm going to hang up now."

"Don't you want to know what kind of bad things?"

"I know your idea of bad. You like to dominate me."

"And you like it. Come on, Pepper, you like when I make suggestions. You can't help that it turns you on."

"You are out of your tiny little mind."

He laughed again, the sound sending jolts of electricity through her body. "Hey, Pepper, what are you wearing?"

"None of your business. God, don't look like that."

"Like what? Is the camera back on me?"

"Like you do when, oh, never mind. Yes, the camera is watching you again, and I can read your lips."

"Really, what color are your panties?" He ducked his head, pulling the brim of his cap low to cover his face. "Are they pink? I love those pink lace panties that cup your ass and…"

"Jaime, stop it."

"When you tell me what color your panties are."

She sighed. "Fine. They are pink. There, are you happy?"

"No, they aren't. You lied to me, Pepper. Now, I want you to unzip your shorts and tell me for real and for true what color they are."

"You're pure evil. You do know that, don't you?"

"Yeah, but you like me this way. Do it, Pepper. I dare you."

"Fine, if it'll shut you up." She wiggled in her seat holding the phone so that he could hear her zipper. She eased her shorts off and damn... "They're aqua."

"I am flattered. You're wearing team colors, Pepper. That's my girl."

"Can I go now?"

"Now, baby, don't get mad. I'm just playing with you." He looked up at the camera.

She could see the devil in his eyes. Then he smiled that smile that sent shivers down her spine.

"Don't do that."

"Don't do what?"

"Look at me like that. You look like you know what I look like naked."

"But I do know what you look like naked,

Pepper. And I know what you sound like when you're turned on. And, baby, right now you are doing that little breathless thing you do."

"I am not."

"You are too; are you wearing a bra?"

"Why do you always ask me that?"

"Just answer the question."

"No." Damn she didn't want him to know that. She could see his jaw move into a grin, though she couldn't see his face as the camera panned past him again. "I'm wearing your T-shirt and panties. There are you happy?"

"Oh God, Pepper. You're killing me dead, baby. Are your nipples hard?"

"We are not having phone sex, Jaime, especially when I can see you on national television."

"But that's what makes it fun. Pinch your nipples for me, baby. I want to hear that sound you make."

"Ooh, Jaime. Ooh, that feels great. There, now

does that make you happy?"

"That's not the sound I mean. Pinch your left nipple. Pepper. That one is more sensitive. Come on, baby. Do it for me."

"I hate you," she said into the phone. His laugh caressed her making her skin tingle.

Before she could stop herself, she did as he asked. Her nipple turned hard as she pinched, divine sensation coursed through her body.

"Oh yeah, baby, that's the sound. Sort of a throaty moan that turns into a purr. I love that sound, Pepper. I love the taste of your nipples. Did you know that?"

"No." Sanity had abandoned her as wanton need set in. His voice like a drug that she craved she cupped her breast squeezing her nipple as his voice licked her. "That feels good, Jaime."

"I know it does, baby. You sound so good. I want to climb through this phone, take your panties off, and lick your pretty clit. Would you like that, Pepper?"

"Yes, Jaime, oh yeah. That would be wonderful. I want your hot mouth on me." Damn it, she shook her head, trying to force the miasma of hot molten need away, but his laugh undid her.

"Slip your finger inside your panties, baby. I want you to come for me." The camera was full on him now, he leaned his elbows on his knees his head low as he spoke to her. She could see the muscles in his forearms clench and relax. Damn, but she loved those arms, all sleek and tan.

"I love your arms. Did you know that? Your muscles make me weak." God help her, she slid her hand down her belly and inside her panties. Warm, wet heat greeted her finger as she tentatively touched her clit.

"Oh, baby, you sound so sweet. Does that feel good? Pretend your finger is my tongue."

"That feels so good, Jaime, ooh…"

"Open your legs for me baby, slide your finger lower. Oh, Pepper, you sound so good. Purr for me baby. Go inside, deeper."

She opened her legs, lifting one onto the couch as she sank deeper into the cushion and angled her hips as she stroked her clit letting her finger slide inside her pussy.

"Jaime, I need you," she whispered as he coaxed her to add a second finger. "I want you inside me."

"Come for me, Cass. Now, baby. I'm running out of time. Come for me. Stroke your clit, baby, just underneath it. Pretend I'm there with you. Pretend I'm inside you. You feel so creamy, Cass, hot and tight. And I'm pushing into you. Short, hard thrusts. I know you like when I fuck you like that. I'm thrusting faster now, Pepper. Oh yeah, baby, that's the sound I love. Come for me, Pepper."

"I'm…oh God. Jaime, that feels so damn good. I want you deep inside me, just like that." She slid her fingers in deep, arching against them as he instructed her. Short, fast thrusts that had her panting. Orgasm started in her toes. Her legs shook from exertion.

Pleasure washed through her just as he looked up at the camera, his eyes intense, his face almost hard with concentration. As he watched her from the television, she burst sky high.

"That's my girl. Goddamn, Pepper, that was nasty." She heard him say through the haze that crowded into her mind.

"I still hate you."

He just laughed again, "I know you do. Come home, Pepper. I miss you hating me to my face."

"Tomorrow," she promised, hating herself even as the words tumbled from her lips.

"I'll catch the first flight out tomorrow."

She watched his face light up, and then he turned to look at something down the field. "Got to go now, Pepper. I'll see you tomorrow." And he was gone, the announcers still talking about the long phone call, wondering who he was really talking to. Cass turned off the television after he put his helmet on. She felt dirty and used and incredibly sated all at the same time. She wouldn't give him the pleasure of knowing she was watching him play after that dirty trick. Instead, she went to check flight availability and pack. Tomorrow, when she got home, she would kick his ass for being a prick and treating her as if she was property. Then she looked at the front of the T-shirt she was wearing, and for the first time she understood what he found so funny the last time she'd worn it.

Property number 4 Miami Football.

The aqua number against a stark white jersey blazed across her memory. He was fucking number four.

"Son of a *bitch*!" she shouted and stalked off to her room to find something else to wear while she plotted his murder.

Chapter Sixteen

Chicago fell that evening to the well-oiled machine Jaime knew his team was. Everything went according to plan. He was untouchable. They were untouchable.

Excitement coursed through his veins. He was the happiest, luckiest man to ever walk the face of the earth, and no damn Bear was going to get in his way.

After the game, the ribbing began, starting with the press who wanted to know who he'd called before the game. He just smiled and evaded the question. His fifteen-minute conversation with Pepper was nobody's business but his own. It continued into the locker room, but he let it all wash over him. They'd won and would continue winning. It didn't matter who gave him the pregame pep talk.

He spent the evening with a group of players and their wives at a club on the beach just watching his men have fun. Colas and water were all he drank, keeping to himself or with his people to avoid the groupies. He took some ribbing for that too. Not long ago, he'd been the first to dive head first into the fray, but too much had changed this past year.

"Where's your little brunette friend?" A blonde with a man-made rack sat across from him. He couldn't remember who she was here with, one of the running backs probably.

"Baby, Jay doesn't like brunettes, especially little ones." Miguel Donham, his best running back, scooted in beside Jaime. "Ain't that right, Jay?" Jaime just smiled and swirled the ice in his cola, but something in her eyes had his attention. How exactly did she know about Pepper?

"I've seen him with one, baby. Sort of petite with a cute face and hair so dark it's almost black.

Once just riding by on the street, while I was jogging and again at this club, a little while back. She had the most incredible blue eyes I've ever seen."

"You know a woman like that, Jay?" Another teammate sat down and draped his arm across the blonde's shoulders.

"Maybe. What if I do?" The three of them just stared him down. "She's a friend, all right?"

"Yeah, man, friend with benefits. I get you, Jay. The way you've been playing these past few weeks, those must be some damn good benefits." Jaime felt his skin grow tight, his arm muscles clenched and unclenched.

"Whoa, hey man, put the devil stare away. I didn't mean anything by it. Jeezus Christ, man, how do you do that with your eyes anyway? No wonder people are afraid of you," Miguel said. "Sorry, I didn't mean to hit a nerve. I mean, whatever it is, man, that's got you walking on air out there on the field, then you have my blessing.

Keep it up.

Okay, put the guns away. I don't want to get into anything in public, and we sure as hell can't afford a suspension right now."

He made himself relax. His shoulder that ached from a couple of bad hits, didn't like being misused right now. "Her name is Pepper. She really is just a friend, so keep your nasty thoughts to yourself."

"I don't know. That night the two of you looked a whole lot more than just friends to me." The blonde said, taking a sip of her drink. Her eyes grew wide when he turned his stare on her.

"Hush, baby. If Jay says she's just a friend, then that's what she is—whatever keeps Jay happy. If he wants to make mysterious phone calls from the field to talk to his friend, then that's his bidness. Maybe we could all take a few minutes for a little pregame phone sex. You think that might work, baby? I call you up and you talk dirty to me." Jaime'd had enough. He set his drink down, and with a carefully guarded good night, drove himself home. Alone and on edge, he roamed the house much as he had every night for the past week. The quiet was deafening.

He settled in his office, trying not to remember that night a couple of weeks ago and the things he'd done to her on his desk. He checked his messages — none were from her — and then went online. He wanted to call her as he had every night this week, listen to her talk about her day, and let her tease him about being a stupid jock. Several times he'd come so close to telling her how much he missed her.

His phone buzzed, but it wasn't her calling. Just a text message to let him know she was on the ten o'clock flight out of Birmingham and wishing him a good night, oh, and congratulations on the win.

He didn't call her. He wanted to so badly he could feel it in his teeth. The week caught up with him sometime around one, and he climbed the stairs alone; stopping on the landing, he turned toward her room instead of his own. Her sheets were softer. He stripped to his skin and crawled into her bed, letting her scent wrap around him until he drifted into sweet oblivion.

*****

Her flight was late. He walked the concourse at the airport waiting and trying to look as inconspicuous as possible. He'd been recognized a couple of times but so far no mob scenes. When her flight flashed on the screen as arrived, he relaxed and waited for her to clear the gate. Only then did he release the breath he hadn't realized he was holding.

She had her hair pulled back in a loose braid that hung over her shoulder. She looked tired when he first laid eyes on her. Then she found him standing at the back of the crowd, and her eyes lit up, her mouth stretched into a grin. He smiled back, enjoying the blush that traveled from her face down her neck to disappear beneath her blouse. Pepper did everything whole-heartedly. He knew her breasts would be just as rosy as her face.

"Hey, are you incognito?" She walked up to him and shrugged her carry-on bag off her shoulder. "I would think the crimson hat with a big white A on it would be the last thing you'd choose."

"Well, it was this or a New England hat. I don't think anyone would appreciate that, do you?" He had explained that he spent his first three years in the NFL sitting on the Pat's bench, but she still looked at him as if he'd lost his mind. "I don't have many hats, okay? So, uh, how was your vacation?"

"Well, I discovered that my mother has a wild streak and is living a more exciting life than I am. I think she has a boyfriend. I caught her sneaking in one night after two. I have to apologize to you now because unfortunately she and her Red Hat syndicate shanghaied your mother and took her off to Tunica yesterday. To the best of my knowledge, the whole blamed pack is still over there. And I heard something about a strip joint last night. Oh Lord. It's good to be back around the sane and the boring. Stop laughing, that pack of gray-hairs is wild. Your mom is being corrupted."

"I'd forgotten how much you talk." He stopped her by lifting her chin and pressing his lips to hers. "So how was the flight? Did you puke?"

"I didn't puke, thank you very much. Thought about it for the first hour, but a glass of champagne helped settle my stomach."

"That was what, your sixth flight? I think you might be getting the hang of it."

"Fifth," she said once they stood beside his car. "That was my fifth time in a plane. And I think I might want you to kiss me again."

"Oh really. What if I don't want to?"

"Then I'll just flash my panties, and you'll do

anything I want you to do. Now, Jaime Dalton, kiss me before I do something drastic like pass out."

"How much wine did you say you'd had?"

"Just the one. Why do you ask?"

"No reason." She lifted her head automatically, smiling into his eyes as he leaned her against his car. "You smell like vanilla. Just getting close to you makes me want to lick you like an ice-cream cone."

"You can lick me later. Right now, I'm going to die if you don't kiss me. Please, Jaime, I've dreamed of your lips on mine every night, it seems."

"After you call me Lord Ironman."

"You really are incorrigible, you know that, right?"

"Sticks and stones, baby, now call — You have to earn that kiss. Say it."

"Lord Ironman, please play tonsil hockey with me, just this one time. There, does that make you happy?"

"Ecstatic. Pucker up, baby, I'm diving in."

Her lips were soft and sweet. Her tongue met his eagerly, and what should have been just a tender peck on the lips became heated way too fast. His body responded in kind. He pressed her hard against the car, her little moans of pleasure rapidly becoming seductive purrs. "Dammit, Pepper, remind me to buy something with a big back seat and limousine-tinted windows."

"Jaime you need a bigger car so we can make out in parking lots."

"You are mouthy when you're horny."

"I'm mouthy all the time."

"Just get in the car. The faster we get home, the faster I can give you a proper welcome."

"Promise."

"Note to Pepper. Lay off the champagne or walk around naked. It's your only choice from now on."

"Bite me, Jaime. Oh wait, you usually do."

"Just get in the damned car or I am going to snag your panties and do you right here against the car in broad daylight. Do you want that?"

"Let me think about it."

"Pepper, you are killing me."

"So you keep telling me."

Mercy Celeste

Chapter Seventeen

For the next three weeks, Cass was on top of the world. That day after her vacation, they didn't make it past the stairs before he had her naked and crying out his name. Jaime had all but moved into her room. The nights he didn't sleep with her were the nights he was away.

The first part of the week after training camp was over, Jaime stayed home. Needless to say, very little work got done on those two or three days. She stopped bothering with clothes at all. One of his loose T-shirts proclaiming her his property was all she needed those days.

The latter part of the week, he was gone more than he was home. Two more Saturday games took him out of town for most of the weekend. In those weeks, she finally found a dining room table. True to Jaime's prediction, there was something else to use one for besides dining. Unless of course, he considered her to be the main course.

Sometimes she wondered if he did.

There were no more packages, no threatening letters, and after a second visit from a forensics team, no police questions. Just her, him, and sexual debauchery. She'd even gotten used to calling him Lord Ironman when it suited her purposes.

Then the regular season reared its ugly head. Jaime got her passes for the first game Sunday night against the Packers. That she was nervous about actually going to the game was an understatement. She had never been to a football game in her life, not even in high school. After she asked him what to wear for the tenth time, he took her up to bed, stripped her naked, and made her forget such a thing as football even existed. When he finally untied her from the headboard, he had an entire outfit laid out.

A pair of low-waisted jeans and a skintight Miami T-shirt that he'd picked up from the team store that week. "No panties. I want to know you're sitting up there in the stands commando."

"Well, for fuck's sake, Jaime, why don't I just go naked?"

"That's a great idea. But you're too chickenshit to show your goodies to the world."

"Why do I have this incredible urge to murder you?"

"Again? Baby, you really do need to get these violent tendencies under control."

"Oh, go jump off the balcony or something."

"Can't I help you dress?"

"God, Jaime, it takes too long to get dressed when you help. Don't you have somewhere to be this afternoon?"

"You do have a point. Okay, so I'm going to go down to the kitchen and find something to eat while you get dressed. And Pepper, if you have to wear panties, at least wear the aqua ones."

"How about the coral ones, combination of pink and team pride?"

"Baby, I like the way you think." He kissed her on the small of her back and walked out of the room, his clothes still lying in a heap on the floor beside her bed. Their bed.

She lay there shivering despite the warm noonday sun streaming in through the windows. Somehow over the past few weeks, this had become their room and she'd been too busy loving the things he did to her to notice something as monumental as two lives entwining to become one.

She wasn't a fool. Jaime still kept his things in his own room. His life was still his own. It was her life that had become his. She belonged to him in body and soul while he was still a free agent who wasn't about to turn down free sex.

God damn him and the horse he rode in on.

Several hours after he left to go psych himself

up to whip some Packer ass, Cass stepped out of the limo he'd arranged to take her to the stadium. Cameras flashed around her; the scene was rowdy, electric, but security hustled her past all of that and into the stadium leading her to a boxed area very close to the field.

The section seemed to be solely populated by women and children with a sprinkling of some older couples. She looked them over in much the same way they looked her over.

Open curiosity, and on her part, terror at being under such close scrutiny. "Who's your player, hon?" An older woman stepped out of the seats holding out her hand. "You look brand-new and scared to death. Which one of the rookies are you here to cheer on?"

"Uh, number four, but I don't think he's a rookie," Cass stammered; she really was out of her comfort zone here.

"You're Jay's guest. Well, hon, how about that. Sometimes, Miz Dalton comes to watch him play, and well, there was that one…"

Another woman came to her rescue. The resemblance to the first one was remarkable in that they both had white blonde hair styled high and sprayed to form a sort of helmet of curls. With the same drawling accent they could have been twins except for the age difference. "Taylor, gawd, there is no need to bore her to death. Come on in, sweetie. I'm Trish and this is my bestie, Taylor. We're from Dallas, not like you couldn't tell. Come sit with us. Tell us all about you and how you know Jay."

"Well." How much did she need to tell them? The better question would be how much did Jaime want her to tell them? "I'm Pep—I'm Cass Pendleton, I'm Jay's … y'all call him Jay?"

"Yeah, honey, Jay, short for Jamison. What do you call him?" Trish asked; at least Cass thought it was Trish.

"Mr. Pendleton."

"Well, don't that just beat all?" Taylor's light

brown eyes turned up in a wicked grin.

"I sometimes call my Tater down there Mr. Sandborne, too. Come on, honey, what do you really call him when he's pissed you off?"

"Besides jerk, I call him Jaime. But you have it all wrong, I am not—" Yes, she was. Lord, how did one go about denying that a non-existent relationship existed without looking like a fool? "I work for Jaime, that's all. Sort of like a Girl Friday."

"Uh-huh, hon. Most of us worked for our man in one form or another too. So come on, sit down. It's a long time until kickoff, and we want to get to know all about you." Shit, Cass was afraid Taylor was going to say something like that. "Well, what do you want to know?" Ooh, really bad mistake.

The section began to fill up as game time neared. Cass found herself surrounded by curious women, all of them wanting to know everything about her and how she met Jay.

She told them as close to the truth as she was

willing to tell. She grew up in the same small Alabama city Jaime did, and that he found her through a temp agency in the spring.

That they were friends and nothing more.

Of course, the little knowing looks were passed from one to the other with coos of yeah, um-hm, just friends, smirk, smirk, wink, wink. A guy with a tray of beer walked by and Cass snagged one. Never mind that she hated beer or that she really never could handle her alcohol; the stress of being in the crosshairs was more than she could stand sober.

Just as she was about to take her first drink, her phone rang. She knew it was him without looking at the phone. He sat on a bench not far from her, hunched over. "Hey, where are you?" he said, his voice low and husky.

"Turn around and look up." He stood up, turning until he was facing her. He smiled, looked at the curious faces surrounding her, and quickly sat back down.

"So you go by Jay, now?"

"How much have they told you? Better yet, how much have you told them? Okay, I don't want to know. So, are you wearing panties?"

"You'll have to wait to find out."

"Come on, Pepper. Don't be mean."

"Hey, I'm sitting up here surrounded by all these women listening intently to this conversation. I'd love to chat with you, but I don't think … oh shit." She saw herself on the scoreboard. "Why am I on that screen?"

Jaime looked up, saw her just before it cut to him. "They're just speculating. You're on the phone, I'm on the phone, and I just stood up and looked for you."

"You know, now may not be the time to discuss this, but we might need to define this thing between us sooner or later. Eww, that's nasty."

"What's nasty?" His sat up straight, looking around as if something had happened that he couldn't see.

"This beer, it's awful."

"Why are you drinking beer, Pepper? You hate beer."

"I know. I'm just sort of hoping to get buzzed, so I get through this without puking." He laughed. "Booze makes you horny, Pepper. Are you going to be ready for me when this is all over? I'll find us a place somewhere nice and quiet where I can find out if you're wearing panties."

"You know there is a boatload of good-looking men sitting around me. What if I decided I like one of them better than you?"

"Damn, Pepper, you're wicked. Pick one out, bring him home. Just promise me I can watch, okay?"

"Jaime, Christ, stop laughing, we are not having … we aren't even talking about that. I do have some scruples."

"I don't."

"So I understand. Really, you'd watch me

with another guy?" He didn't answer. She could see his back go rigid, then he stood up and faced her.

There was no laughter in his eyes that she could see. "No. I'd kill anyone who touched you."

He was dead serious. She could see it all over his body. Heat washed though her body; a lump formed in her throat. "I'm not wearing panties." He smiled then and pointed to her. "That's my girl," he said softly, but she read his lips. "Oh, hey, got to go. Don't get drunk, Pepper. I like you sober when I molest you."

"As you command, Lord Ironman."

"Damn straight." He hung up, winked up at her, grabbed his helmet, and went to work.

"Well, I guess that mystery is solved." Taylor leaned in close, her eyes narrow slits.

"Don't worry, honey. When this is over, we'll get you out of here before the press finds you."

"What? Why would the…" Cass followed Taylor's pointed finger to the scoreboard that was just now replaying Jaime's point and his mouthed words, "That's my girl," and her blushing reaction. "Oh shit."

*****

"Oh shit!" Cass cringed with each hit, the sound almost like two cars colliding. Jaime took his fair share, but the players around him protected him for the most part.

Still, even when it wasn't Jaime, the sound of plastic hitting plastic was enough to make the mostly forgotten beer come back up.

The air was charged as the men roared and shouted and cussed and cheered from the sidelines. The crowd was even louder than they were. Bodies flew into the air, only to get up and run away with huge grins on their faces. The women around her screamed, cussed, and promised to kill whoever had just tossed their beloved into the air. All Cass could do was hold on to her seat every time Jaime was the body flung about as if he were little more than a rag doll.

She relaxed some during halftime, finding the stomach to grab a burger and a Coke from concessions.

"You haven't been to too many games have you, hon?" Trish, the other half of the Texas twosome, cornered her in the restroom.

"This is my first. Is it that obvious?"

"Sort of. Look, hon, I'm not going to lie to you. It's tough watching them take the hits, but after a while you'll get used to it. They train for this, and the equipment is state of the art, you know."

"But it's so brutal."

"Sure, it's brutal; that's why it's fun to watch. Come on, hon, you're doing great, one more half to go."

"Out of how many more games?"

Trish just laughed and patted her on her back. "By the end of the season you'll be immune, you'll see. Let's head back. The third quarter is about to start." The game slowed down in the fourth quarter. Miami was trailing by three points, and it became a game of just moving the ball instead of long passes. Stop and start, time out after time out, while they plotted how best to take the lead from the Packers.

Jaime was a man on fire, his eyes alive as he screamed and roared. Trying to keep momentum up, as the clock was winding down, he took a snap from the center. With three long strides back, he looked around for someone to throw to. Then, he pulled his arm back and threw a long arching pass that had everyone in the stadium on his or her feet.

All eyes traveled with the ball, except for Cass. She only had eyes for Jaime, and the two Packer linemen who were barreling toward him.

Jaime's feet were still in the air when the biggest one plowed into him from down low; the other one caught him in the chest, the sound much like a freight train. Cass was on her feet. Her heart plummeted to her stomach. His body flew high in the air, his feet flew over his head, and somehow his helmet came off and flew in the other direction.

Almost as if she were watching a slow-motion replay, Cass stood helplessly by while the crowd erupted in victorious cheers, just as Jaime landed hard, his shoulder and neck taking all of his weight. His helmet continued to roll past the fifty-yard line, but he just lay there in a heap, unmoving, as the clock ticked down to zero.

"We won, hon. We won." One of the Texas twosome grabbed her, but she broke free.

"Jaime!" she screamed, pointing to his motionless body just lying there, no one coming to his aid.

A hush fell over the stadium. Coaches began pouring out onto the field. The other players stopped celebrating. Even the other team stopped and stood like yellow and green statues as the hit Jaime took was played on the screen above their heads. He still didn't move.

Cass felt an arm snake around her shoulder.

"It's going to be all right. He's okay, hon. It's going to be all right." The women gathered around her holding her up when she felt her knees give out.

But it wasn't all right. A camera from above the field came to rest over his seemingly lifeless body, showing the medical team scrambling to wake him up. He didn't cooperate.

After several long moments, a stretcher was brought out and Jaime's neck immobilized.

One of the water boys picked up his helmet and held it close. She could see horror in his young eyes.

The announcers spoke over the crowd, trying to get word of his condition. Referees consulted and reviewed the play. Then it was as if time sped up. Jaime was loaded onto a golf cart, and still unconscious, driven into the heart of the stadium, presumably to the ambulance on standby.

The security guard who had escorted her in showed up at her elbow, startling her. "Miss

Pendleton, you need to come with me."

"Oh God," was all she could think over and over and over.

"Come on, hon, I'll walk with you." One of the Texas ladies grabbed her around her waist.

"Ma'am, if you don't mind, I have to get you down below as quickly as possible. Miss Taylor, I don't have room on the cart for you. Come on, Miss Pendleton, we need to hurry."

"Call me Pepper." She let him take her arm, and then they broke into a run. The concourse cleared for the security cart he barreled through twisting and turning hallways until she was lost and confused. The scene in the locker room was bedlam. The players were still on the field, waiting for news. The medical team gave over to the EMTs. She could feel the tension and fear as she walked into the room. The drone of a helicopter made her heart skip too many beats to count.

"Pepper."

Her knees threatened to give out. He said her

name a second time, and she stuffed her knuckles into her mouth to stop the sob from escaping. "I'm here, baby. I'm here."

"Good." He smiled a weak smile, his eyes swimming with pain. "Hey, Pepper, I guess I'm not Ironman after all."

"You just need the proper armor, Jaime. That's all."

"That's good to know. Hey, did we win?"

She looked around at one of the people in a Miami uniform who nodded. "Yeah, baby, you won."

"Good. Stay with me, Pepper."

"Nothing can stop me, Jaime. Nothing."

"Let's go." One of the EMTs grabbed her by the elbow, and they ran out just as the helicopter landed. Seconds later, they were flying over the lights of the stadium and into the dark night. Jaime's warm hand in hers was the only thing keeping her from having a total breakdown.

Chapter Eighteen

She walked the long hallway outside radiology with her stomach in knots. So far, they knew for certain that his shoulder was dislocated on impact. Possible rib fracture, neck and spinal injury, and concussion were on the list to rule out. That he'd stayed unconscious for so long swayed heavily toward concussion. She waited along with a member of the coaching staff for news. Jaime's mom on the phone kept her company.

"Yes'm, he is awake and talking. They have him immobilized, but he held my hand, and he says his chest hurts when he breathes. Yes'm, that is a good sign. He's in MRI now, but you know hospitals—they forget there are people worrying. I know the footage is horrifying, him lying in a twisted heap like that. Yes'm, you're on the first flight in the morning. I'll be there. Yes'm, I'll be here all night. I'll let you know as soon as they tell me anything."

After she hung up with Jaime's mother, Cass's mother called. Her worry was about Cass first and Jaime second. Cass was able to calm her down and promised her she would call her the second she heard anything. When she was finally able to disconnect, Cass turned her phone completely off and went and sat beside the coach.

"His mom? Man, I don't envy you that call." Marcus Wells, the offensive line coach took her hand in his and patted it almost as if she were a little dog. He was older, but not old, somewhere between forty and fifty; large, like most ex-football players of that age were; and almost jovial.

"I grew up with Jaime. His mom and my mom were friends. She's a nice lady. God, I hated hearing the fear in her voice. All of the news networks are running the footage.

She's scared out of her mind that he's

paralyzed, or heck, I'm not even sure what is running through her mind at this point."

"Well, what did you call him? Jaime? Jaime, I like that better than Jay. Makes him a little more human." He laughed, and she knew that if Jaime made it back out onto the field, he was in for a world of trouble. "Jaime is tough. If his helmet hadn't gone flying, he wouldn't have been knocked out. It's the neck and shoulder. How much damage? Will he need surgery? The concussion is the least of our worries right now, to be honest. A spinal injury can end his career tonight."

"Well, thanks for that. I am so relieved."

He laughed again. "You seem like you have a brain on your shoulders. He knows who we all are, and he can move his hands. He is complaining very loudly about being trussed up like a Thanksgiving turkey. Sounds like he's probably fine to me. How about you?"

"Sure, Jaime is tough. He's going to be just

fine. Probably drive me crazy while he's recovering. Pepper, get me this. Pepper, what's to eat? Pepper…" She stopped talking when the technician and attending doctor stepped into the hallway, their faces grim as they talked. Dread clamped hold of her stomach and wouldn't let go.

"Well, Doc, what are we looking at?" Marcus rose to greet him, his voice going from teasing to determined.

"Concussion, definitely, there doesn't seem to be any damage to his spine. The shoulder is going to be his worst problem. We'll fix that and immobilize it. Two cracked ribs. His temperature is fine, so really we're just going to admit him for a day or two. If he rests and gives his body a chance to heal, he should be fine."

"How long does he need?" The coach seemed relieved. "I'll bench him for as long as it takes."

"He's not going to like that." Pepper shook her head, pity in her voice. "I don't envy you that conversation."

"Oh, I'm not crazy, I'm going to tell him while they still have him trussed up, and then I'm going to run like hell. You're probably the one who's going to have to deal with the fallout."

"Yeah, well, thanks for that."

"One week, maybe two, but we'll make that decision later in the week." The doctor raised an eyebrow at their byplay.

"Thanks, Doc." Marcus shook his hand just as Jaime was wheeled into the hallway.

"Hey there, killer. You look pretty good for a paraplegic."

"I am not in the mood for your jokes, Mark. Just give it to me straight, and I won't kill you when I get up from here." There was no humor in his voice, only pain.

"Okay, it's bad. I'm putting you on the injured list for at least a week. If you take it easy and let that shoulder heal and don't knock that thick skull of yours up any worse than it already is, we'll talk more in a week."

"So I'm benched, then." He wasn't happy about it. Injury or not, Jaime wasn't going to miss a game easily.

"One game, Jaime. Do what the doctors and this nice young lady tell you to do for the next week, and we'll see if you're going out to Dallas in a couple of weeks." Marcus stopped kidding around and made sure Jaime understood before he drew in a deep breath.

"Okay, I'm going to go talk to the press now. Wish me luck. And Pepper, take care of yourself. Don't let him push you around."

"His mama is coming in tomorrow, so that shouldn't be a problem, sir."

"Don't call me sir, honey. Just Mark will do. Jaime, be good, or I'll have the whole offensive line come and babysit you." He leaned over, placed a kiss on her cheek, and ran off down the hallway.

"What a nice man." She stepped beside Jaime as the orderlies wheeled him slowly down the hallway.

"Nice man, my ass. He's a sadist. Why did you have to go and tell him my childhood nickname? Now I'm never going to hear the end of it."

"You know, I think I like you tied up like this, but I can do without the sass, young man."

"Bite me, Pepper."

"If you are really, really nice to me, Jaime Dalton, I might let you bite me."

* * * * *

Sometime after midnight, Jaime was finally settled into a private room, this time only half trussed up like a turkey. His neck was at least out of the cage, and he could use his left arm, but that was about as free as he was going to get for a while at least.   "Are you in pain?" The nurse fussed with warm blankets and making sure he was safely wrapped in a vented gown.

"If I said I wasn't in pain, could I go home?" he growled back at her. "And no fucking needles.

I don't need or want anything dripping into me."

"Someone is cranky tonight." Pepper walked in on the end of the exchange and shoved a phone at him. "Here, your mom wants to talk to you." He gave her his best go-to-hell look, but she wouldn't run. He liked her better when she was afraid of him. She shoved the phone again, and this time he took it, offering up a long-suffering sigh before he put it to his ear. "Hey, Mama. Yeah, I'm going to be just fine. They gave me something nice to help with the pain, but they won't let me sleep, so I don't see what the point is. I am not being rude to the staff. Or Cass either. Yes, I know I'm lucky to have a woman like her taking care of me."

"He's rolling his eyes," Cass said very loudly. "And being rude to the nice nurse standing beside him."

"Pepper, do you mind? I'm talking to my mother. Can't you go find me something to eat or something?"

"And he's starving. He's going to be just fine," she said just before she disappeared into the bathroom.

"Yeah, Mama. Cass is a living doll, and I need to stop treating her badly. I know. Really, Mom, it's not necessary. All right, I'll see you tomorrow. I love you too." The nurse set Cass's phone on the nightstand beside her purse as she went around closing the blinds. "Is your lady staying with you tonight?"

"I've tried to send her home, but she won't go, so I guess she's sleeping in that chair over there," he answered, secretly relieved not to have to spend the next few hours of forced wakefulness alone.

"I'll bring her a pillow and a blanket, then." She handed him the TV remote and the buzzer to the nurse's station, explained how they worked, and said that someone would be in to check on him every so often. "Buzz, if you need anything."

"Is it too late for dinner? I have a sudden

craving for turkey."

"I ordered a pizza. You'll just have to manage on just one. And you're cleaning it up, if it comes back up." Pepper chose that moment to walk back into the room. She dropped wearily into the uncomfortable-looking hospital chair.

"You certainly have thought of everything." He didn't mean for it to come out sounding cranky.

"Well, no. If I'd thought of everything, I'd have something more comfortable to sleep in besides jeans and a too-tight T-shirt. I'd have brought a book, too, but I probably won't be able to read with all the whining."

"I am not whining. I'm hungry and I can't move my arm and I'm wearing a gown that opens in the back."

She just rolled her eyes at him. "And a toothbrush. I would have definitely brought a toothbrush."

"Pepper." He drew her name out, hoping

she'd take the warning.

"Jaime," she mimicked as she kicked her shoes off and wiggled her toes. "God, that feels so much better. What were you saying, your lord highness? I wasn't listening."

"I'm sorry I scared you," he said after the nurse bustled out of the room. "I had plans for tonight that didn't involve an MRI machine."

"I'm sure you had plans that involved some sort of bondage and nudity." She laughed pointedly at his bound arm.

"Well, I guess we're halfway there. If you'd take pity on me and strip, then I'm sure we could salvage the evening."

"Mmm. Do you know what kind of liquor this hospital serves? Because, Lord Ironman, it's going to take a whole lot of booze to get Pepper Potts naked and in bed with you after the night she's had." She closed her eyes, her voice becoming soft and dreamy.

"Hey, Pepper, wake up. If I can't sleep, neither

can you." She opened one eye and smiled at him. "When the pizza comes. Until then I need a few to recharge. Deal?"

"Deal," he said, just as the nurse came back in carrying a stack of blankets and two pizza boxes. "Hey, Pepper, the pizza is here."

"Oh, fuck you," she said irritation ringing in her voice, but she sat up anyway. She looked too pale, too tired. He knew in that moment that he'd never seen anyone as beautiful as Cass, even if the glare in her blue eyes was telling him exactly where to stick himself.

"In your dreams, honey. In your dreams."

Somehow, Pepper managed to carry on a half-coherent conversation until around two, when she fell asleep sitting in the chair.

"Pepper," he called out to her. "Cass. Wake up."

She sat up quickly, her eyes barely in focus. "I'm awake. Are you all right? Do you need anything?"

"Cass, why don't you come lay beside me, baby? You're breaking my heart." He pulled the blankets up and with a little effort scooted over against the rail. "Come on, Pepper, before you fall on your face."

"I don't want to hurt you." She sat there listing sleepily in the chair, her speech slightly slurred.

"You won't hurt me. Take your jeans off, baby, and come lie with me." Too tired to argue, she looked at the door, and within seconds, she stripped out of her jeans, a pair of pink panties clearly visible below her short T-shirt. She carefully climbed into the narrow bed with him and curled against his uninjured side. Sleep snatched her before he could tuck the blanket around her shoulders, her hand resting lightly on his chest. "That's my girl."

He spent the next hour flipping through the pitiful selection of sports news channels while Cass lay on his shoulder. Watching in horrified fascination the double hit that he'd never seen coming. The cuts to Cass standing in the seats while he lay motionless on the ground had his heart racing. The two Texas T's supporting her seemed to be the only thing keeping Cass on her feet. She had her hand pressed over her mouth; her eyes filled with pain as he continued to lie there.

Ten minutes. He was out for ten minutes before being taken off the field. Damn. The entire stadium was silent for that entire ten minutes.

His throw just as time ran out was good, despite the hit he took. Cut to Marcus Wells speaking to the press waiting downstairs, his relieved face saying more than the words ever could. Hurt but not as bad as it could have been.

Right now, the concussion and the shoulder were their chief concerns. No, there was no discernible spinal damage. He's resting comfortably for now. With at least one game out, possibly two.

He liked Mark. He was a good guy, even though he was a sadist. Cass stirred a bit, rolling more onto her stomach. He winced as she settled; his still sore ribs didn't care for the pressure of her arm, but he'd be damned if he was going to wake her up.

He laid the remote down and gently brushed her hair from her face. She looked so peaceful looking up at him like that, the small smile playing on her lips made him think she knew he was thinking about her. He stroked a strand of her hair between his fingers marveling at how soft it was.

The scent of vanilla lingered in the air, so fresh it was almost as if she'd just stepped from the shower. He loved that smell; it was so … Pepper.

A commotion at the door caught him off guard, a man dressed in scrubs rushed in, the flash from the small camera he wielded blinding in the dim room. Before he could think to grab the buzzer the guy was gone, followed by shouts of stop and running feet.

"Sorry about that; he got past security somehow." The same nurse from earlier stepped into the room, her face flushed with embarrassment. "Are you all right, do you need anything?"

Jaime saw her eyes sweep over Cass's sleeping body and her crumpled jeans on the floor, but she didn't say anything.

"I'm fine. My eyes feel like someone has shoved shards of glass into them, but I'm hanging in."

"No nausea, dizziness, blurred vision, anything like that?"

"Does hungry count?" He offered her a big grin; she smiled, thinking he was kidding. He wasn't kidding; he was starving and it was hours until breakfast. "Out of curiosity, does that door lock? I'd just as soon not have another paparazzi incident before sunup."

"I think we can do something about that." She

looked over Cass again, noting her hair still in his fingers. "Do you need another blanket?"

"Naw, we're good here."

Then she was gone. He could hear the lock catch behind her.

Shit, whatever that prick had managed to capture on that little camera was sure to show up somewhere before the day was out. Shit. Shit. So much for keeping this thing with Cass under wraps. Shit, she was going to be pissed.

* * * * *

Sometime around dawn, Cass began to stir. Her eyes opened slowly, sleep clinging to the edges. Her smile melted his heart.

"Hey," he said, leaning over to kiss her offered lips. "Did you sleep all right?"

"Yeah, I think so. What time is it?" She snuggled against his side, being careful not to jostle him. "You're warm."

"Dawn is all I can tell you. That's based on the pale light coming in from the blinds."

"I have to pick your mother up at the airport at eight. Maybe I should go home and change first." She touched her lips to his in soft tame nips that had his blood boiling.

"Stay for a while longer." He leaned closer toward her, catching her mouth for a deeper kiss. Her tongue touched his, her breath caught in her throat. "I need you, Cass."

"Jaime, we can't. Not here. Someone might walk in."

"The door is locked. The nurses will only come if I call them. Please, baby, make love to me. I need you so much."

"Jaime." Her voice was low. She looked at the drawn curtain that blocked the door from view. "We can't."

Despite her words, she eased the cover off them and slowly straddled his legs. She placed her hands on the pillow on either side of his head, and being careful not to touch him, leaned in for a deeper kiss.

"Don't tease me, Pepper. I've had a bad night. And I want you so badly I can't think straight." He let his free hand settle on her rear end, his fingers toying with the lace that covered her. "Let's take these off."

When she didn't answer, he tugged, which was difficult to do with just one hand.

She took pity on him and tugged the other side to her knees, and then carefully wiggled them on to the bed beside them. "Why is it I can't say no to you?" she whispered beside his ear, her tongue hot on his cheek.

"Because you like the way I make you feel." He eased his fingers between her legs; she moaned prettily when he touched her clit. "You're already wet for me, baby."

"I know. I hate that." She sat up straight, repositioning her hands on the rails for support while he stroked her, sliding a finger deep inside her just to hear her purr. "That feels so good. That gown has to go though. It's in the way." She fiddled with the ties that held the hospital gown closed over his immobilized arm and tossed it to the foot of the bed. She didn't look at the bandaging around his ribs; her eyes centered on that part of him currently in the most pain. She reached out with long fingers, and within seconds, he was gasping.

"Come here." He took her hand, holding it in his while he coaxed her higher in the bed until the heat between her legs all but engulfed him. "Kiss me, Cass." She placed her hands just above his shoulders and rose over him, the head of his cock touching that spot it craved, and with a hitch of her hips he was inside her. Her lips touched his, taking his breath away.

She rode him slowly, gently. Small gasps of pleasure escaped her lips only to be caught by his. Orgasm took her and she leaned back, her arms once again on the rails as her movements became frenzied.

He pushed her top up above her breasts and

somehow, despite the sharp pain in his ribs, he managed to sit up enough to capture her nipples with his teeth, nipping at her through her bra until she shattered around him. She swung her head in a frenzy, trying not to make a sound.

He pressed into her, gently rocking with her as he leaned back against the pillow taking her with him. "That's my girl. I love watching you come, Cass." He cradled her against his body with one arm, his breath coming in gasps as she joined him, grinding against him. He could feel the pulsing between her legs quicken again as a second orgasm built inside her. Her eyes caught his gaze as she held her face close to his. Fire and flame burning in their blue depths. "Jaime…" Her voice caught on a gasp. "I love you."

"I know you do, Cass." He held her to him, the urge to bite strong.

She pulled her shirt off and leaned her head against the pillow. "Bite me, Jaime." He couldn't stop himself; he clamped onto her soft flesh, trying hard not to lose control and break skin, and as he erupted inside her, she cried out his name, which was good because at that precise moment he had no idea who he was.

Chapter Nineteen

"Mr. Dalton, I thought I would let you know that your doctor is starting his rounds." The tinny voice of a nurse over the little intercom interrupted them. Cass heard Jaime reply … something, feeling his voice rumble in his chest as she lay against him, in nothing but her bra, his cock still throbbing deep inside her.

"Pepper, you have to get dressed." She felt him laugh. His hand stroked her hair along her back. Heat swirled in her midsection and dread in her very being. She'd said something monumental that wasn't returned. She was lying mostly naked on an injured man in a hospital bed connected at the crotch after unprotected sex, and all she could find wrong with this situation was that he didn't say he loved her back.

"Shit." She eased off him, keenly aware of the warm stickiness between her thighs.

"Please, remind me to murder you." She grabbed her clothes and ran for the bathroom leaving him to find his own damn gown.

"Come on, Pepper, you can't kill me while I'm hurt. That is like kicking a puppy."

"You're not cute enough to be a puppy. Jesus Christ, Jaime. I have to go pick up your mother smelling like…"

"Smelling like you've been well fucked, Pepper. She already knows we're sleeping together. She won't say anything."

"Did you tell her? Why do you get to tell your mom while I lie to mine?"

"I didn't tell her, and she has never asked me point-blank, but she knows. And so does yours. Baby, come on, it's all right."

"No, it isn't. We didn't have a condom, and I can get pregnant. You should have thought about that before you … you … used me like that." He didn't say anything to that. He looked away when she leaned past the bathroom door. "Listen, Jaime, we can't keep doing this…"

"Close the door, Pepper, before you get caught in your undies by the nursing staff." He cut her off, a tight-lipped smile on his face as she slammed the door. Seconds later, she heard a female voice.

Damn, almost busted. She leaned against the sink, looking at herself in the mirror.

She wore yesterday's makeup; what was left of her eyeliner was smeared, deep dark circles stood out against the paleness of her skin. Her hair was tousled from Jaime's hands, bite marks lined her shoulder, and that was just the damage she could see.

She grabbed a washcloth and ran the water as hot as she could stand, hoping to try to make herself as presentable as she possibly could in yesterday's clothes. But no matter how she tried to shake away the notion, she walked into the room with the dreadful feeling that everyone in the room knew what they had just done in that very bed.

Jaime was speaking with the doctor from the night before while a small team of doctors stood behind them. A different nurse looked curiously at her, making Cass wish the floor would open up and swallow her.

"You remember, Cass, don't you, doctor? She kept me awake. I'm getting ready to send her home so she can sleep and change clothes." The doctor only nodded at her indifferently before he went back to issuing orders for a few additional tests. When he was done, he nodded to her and him, and the whole entourage vacated the room, leaving the incredibly young, blonde nurse behind. Her starstruck eyes were only for Jaime.

"Hey, baby, I need your phone. I can't find mine," he said pointedly to Cass, but the nurse started to answer and stumbled stupidly over the words when she realized he wasn't talking to her.

"Who do you need to call?" She retrieved her phone from the nightstand and checked the time. "It's after seven."

"Franco, to get you a car sent over." He punched the number in, and within minutes, he had Franco himself on his way to pick her up and drive her to the airport.

"Thanks, I'd forgotten I didn't have a ride." She took the phone from him and sat down heavily in the chair while the nurse just stood there watching. "Is it possible you could find Mr. Dalton something to wear besides that gown until I get back with a change of clothes and a toothbrush or something? And I'm sure he's sitting there wondering when breakfast will be served." She spoke to the nurse directly, breaking the starstruck spell. "And when did the doctor say they were going to let him sleep?"

"Oh, soon. They're going to do a couple of tests, and then he can sleep the rest of the day." She looked chagrined but professional now.

"Can I go home to sleep?" Jaime chimed in hopefully from the bed.

"The doctor will make that decision on his evening rounds. Will scrubs be all right?" She spoke directly to Jaime, and Cass took the opportunity to collapse against the chair in exhaustion.

"Those will be great." He looked over at her, and for the first time since she'd come out of the bathroom he looked concerned. "Pepper, do you need the nurse to get you something while she's out? A toothbrush or a sedative or something?"

"A time machine would be very nice. We could set it back to yesterday and none of this would have ever happened. Do you think you could find one of those somewhere?"

"Probably not. I can manage a toothbrush, but I would have to ask a doctor for the sedative." She stood there for a moment and then turned and left.

"How do you think she made it through nursing school?" Jaime cocked one eyebrow.

"Probably on her knees," she said before she could stop herself. His laughter tingled along her spine, making her smile. "That doesn't mean you have permission to find out."

"Aww, look at Pepper, all jealous and territorial. I think I like you like this, Pepper."

"Just remember to remind me that you need seriously killing when we get home," she said, her brain fuzzy and warm with interrupted sleep, the sound of his low laughter soothing.

"Hey, Pepper. Pepper, baby, wake up. Your ride is here." He stood beside her dressed in a pair of dark blue scrub pants, his face very pale, his hair dripping.

"How did you get there? Are you wet?" She sat up, trying to clear her fuzzy mind. A yawn escaped as she stretched.

"You fell asleep while we were talking. I took a few minutes to go wash some of the game off of me, and baby, you really are exhausted. I'll send Franco to the airport while you get some sleep."

"No. No, I promised her I'd meet her. Besides, I need to go home and change so I can be back tonight to bring you home."

"Sleep while you're there, okay, Cass? Promise me you'll stop worrying and sleep." He kissed her forehead and walked her to the door.

"Take care of her, Franco. She's had a tough night. Take her home after you pick up my mom. Okay? Thanks, man, I owe you for getting up so early." Franco just smiled and told Jaime to expect a nice big bill. And that's how she left him. Standing there in a pair of scrubs with his right arm strapped to his side and his ribs bound. For a second, she almost let Franco go on to the airport without her, but the farther away from Jaime she got, the clearer her brain became. And her brain had a few choice words about her recent behavior to impart. In particular, the wisdom that falling in love with Jamison Dalton was probably the biggest mistake she had ever made in her life out of a very long list of mistakes.

She stood out like a sore thumb at the airport. Her Miami T-shirt made her feel as if everyone was staring at her. Jaime's mom spotted her the second she passed through the gate, her arms outstretched, worry clear on her face. "Hey, Miz Dalton. Good morning, did you have a safe flight?"

"It's Helen, honey. Gloria talked the whole way so I was too busy to notice anything else. Oh Lord, honey, you look like death warmed over."

"Cold festering on the side of the road death is how I feel. Wait, what do you mean, Gloria? You don't mean…" Before she even got the words out, her very own mother dressed in a nice linen suit with her hair neatly styled came traipsing out of the gate.

"Mom, what are you doing here?"

"Besides keeping Helen company? I've come to check on you and Jaime and see some of Miami. Don't I get a hug?" She laid down her bag and held her arms out for Cass, who went gratefully into them. "Ew, honey, you stink. We need to get you into a bath and some food in you before you collapse in a heap at our feet."

"But Jaime…" She started to protest that she needed to get home and pack some things to take back to Jaime, but his mother caught her arm and steered her to the baggage claim area.

"Jaime has an entire nursing staff fussing over him, and all he needs right now is sleep. Anything else will just have to wait," Helen said as she hefted a large suitcase off the carousel and went in search of a second one.

"Gee, Helen, did you bring enough with you?" Gloria plucked her single but very large bag out of a pile. "With all the shopping to be done here, you could have left some of it behind."

"They're only half full, how do you think I'm going to haul all those new clothes home, Gloria?" Helen retorted, and for some reason this tickled Cass; she sounded so much like her son it was uncanny.

"I plan to ship everything through the mail. Less to deal with that way," Gloria explained patiently, but Helen just rolled her eyes. "And you, stop laughing. I swear you are the rudest child on the face of the earth."

"I can't help it. You two bicker like an old married couple," Cass couldn't help saying.

"Well, honey, takes one to know one." Helen smiled sweetly and dragging her bag behind her, headed for the door making a beeline to the limo waiting at the curb.

"What did she mean by that?" Cass whispered to her mother as they followed her out.

"Well, Cass, if I have to explain it to you ... on second thought, you wouldn't believe me anyway."

"Exactly how long did you say you were staying?" She rushed out to find Franco lifting Helen's baggage into the trunk.

"A week, maybe two. We're just playing things by ear. Aren't we, Gloria?"

"Oh Lord." Cass climbed in the car and immediately bent down to see if there was anything potent in the bar. It was going to be a very long week or two.

* * * * *

"Hey." Jaime squeezed the hand that held his, the warmth there comforting. His mind was fuzzy from the drugs and sleep, and he ached all over. "How long have you been here?"   "A couple of hours," she said, the voice not the one he expected.

"Did you have a nice flight?" He couldn't focus, but he thought he saw her smile.

"Nice save. I'm not Cass." She always did have a sarcastic streak. He decided he got that from her and not his father.

"I knew that. Where is Pepper anyway? I thought she was coming back with clothes and stuff." He tried to sit up, but his muscles had other ideas.

"Muscle pain finally set in, did it?" She lifted

the blanket and peeked under. "Ooh, those are some pretty bruises. The doctor came while you were sleeping. He's going to let you go home this evening. Not because he wants to, but because you are causing a disturbance."

He winced. "Has she seen it, then?"

"No, we took her home and fed her. Gloria tossed her in the shower, then shoved her into bed. I checked in a little while ago. She was still sleeping."

"She's going to have a freaking cow when she sees it."

"It was a nice picture, Jaime, sweet. However, I can see why it would bother the two of you. You know, sneaking around is not good for a relationship."

"We're not sneaking around. She lives in my house."

"And you sleep in her bed. But you've kept her a secret from the world. I'll bet your teammates don't even know about her. Okay, didn't before the game yesterday at least. And pardon me if I'm prying, but I can't help but wonder if you've even admitted to yourself that you're in a relationship with Cass at this stage."

"Did she say something? Is this why you are harping on this subject?"

"No, Jaime, all Cass did was fret over you. Getting you something comfortable to sleep in. Clothes to come home in. She was worried that the hospital food wouldn't be enough. There was more. She was just going to go in, grab some stuff, and come back here."

"I told her to get some sleep before coming back. I'm sure she put up a fight when you stopped her."

"Not so much. Gloria slipped her a tranquilizer. She didn't even notice, she was so worn out."

He laughed, picturing Pepper falling asleep in the shower. "She's still going to flip when she sees that picture. It's everywhere."

"It made the cover of the sports page this morning. I think I'll frame it. I don't think I've ever seen you so content. Not like…"

"Not like what? Mother, I know you didn't like Lisette…"

"And I was justified in that. Or have you forgotten?"

"But please, don't make more out of this than there is. Cass and I are…"

"Just friends? Is that what you were going to say? Honey, you and Cassandra Pendleton have never been friends. Sexual adversaries since you were both old enough …hell the way the two of you fought when you happened to be in the same room was almost like foreplay as far back as middle school. Everyone knew that but the two of you, apparently. Gloria and I worried most of your high school years that she'd either kill you or turn up pregnant. So don't tell me you're just friends. Friends don't fog up the windows together."

"Mom…" He couldn't think of a thing to say. Pepper had told him she loved him.

This thing had long ago gone past friends with benefits, and he knew it. "I don't want to hurt her."

"Do you love her?"

"Wow, you do get right to the point, don't you? I don't know how I feel about her. She makes me crazy, but Pepper has always made me crazy. I like being with her. She doesn't care about my money or my fame or clothes or stuff. Of course, she doesn't know one damned thing about football, which could be a problem. And she tells me she hates me to my face. How the hell am I supposed to feel about her?"

"Lisette burned you, honey. I understand that. And Cass was there when you pulled your head out of your ass. However, based on what I saw on television last night, and there is that picture of her lying in your arms here in this very bed, all I can say is, you look happy. Don't throw that away just because she doesn't meet some standard you have in that little pea brain of yours."

"Why is it everyone challenges my mentality lately? Doesn't my diploma have magna cum laude on it, or did I dream that up?"

"You know, Jaime, I love you to death, but for a smart man, you certainly are dumb."

"Gee thanks, Mom."

Mercy Celeste

Chapter Twenty

She knew it was still early despite the dark outside her window, but she was too tired to climb out of bed and go downstairs to see what damage those two old biddies had inflicted on her kitchen. Besides, she suspected one of them had drugged her, since she didn't remember much after walking in the door. She sure as hell wouldn't have climbed into bed naked otherwise.

Sleep came and went most of the day. She gave in to it only to be released when she remembered Jaime. Once, she had the television on and could have sworn she'd seen a picture of herself asleep in Jaime's arms—okay, arm, but, after a while, she decided she'd dreamed that.

Her stomach rumbled but she ignored it. She didn't want to leave the warmth of her bed even to answer the call of nature. She could hear them talking downstairs. Two female voices where quiet was supposed to be. There was the scent of food, then dark came. She heard her door open and close gently. The lock clicked into place but she assumed it was her mother. "Move over, Pepper."

She almost sobbed when he settled in beside her, lifting her arm and laying it gently over his chest. "When did you get home? Why didn't someone wake me?"

"Not long ago. You were sleeping so soundly your mom didn't want to disturb you." He wiggled into a comfortable position, grunting with pain when he twisted wrong. "Are you hungry? I brought up a tray."

"Not right now. How are you feeling? What did the doctors say?" She inhaled deeply, taking in his scent. "You smell like hospital soap."

"Sexy, isn't it?" He laughed. "God, you're naked. Kill me now, please."

"I think one of those old ladies down there gave me something. Which one looked guilty?"

"Probably both of them. After all, my mother is a doctor and yours is a nurse. They'd have the nerve and the stuff to do it."

"Your mother is a kindly pediatrician, not a drug moll, so it had to be mine."

"I don't know, Pepper. I have large chunks of my childhood missing thanks to her and her Benadryl supply."

She laughed. She remembered nights in which her mother dosed her too, for allergies she didn't have. "Too bad that stuff doesn't do anything for my actual allergy. Would have saved me a couple of trips to the ER."

"Yeah, after last night, I'd really like to avoid that place for a while. I ache like a sumbitch. They only let me go because of the media circus downstairs."

"Yeah, about that? Who is Lisette? Shit, I don't remember her last name. Is there a picture of us on the news, or did I dream that?"

"No, you didn't dream it. Early this morning, some guy dressed as an orderly got past security and the nurses. He managed to get off a few shots before they almost caught up to him."

"Wow, thanks for the heads up on that, but that doesn't exactly explain this Lisette person?" She noticed he held his breath. "You hold your breath when you don't want to talk about something. All of those commentators were talking about her finding out about the mystery woman in your bed. Why would she care?"

"Lisette Delacroix was my fiancée." He said it very slowly. She could hear something in his voice, shame or hate or whatever.

"Why isn't that little detail on Wikipedia? When was it over? It is over, isn't it?"

"Yeah, it's over. Has been since April. I'm sorry, Cass. I guess I should have at least mentioned her to you."

"You think? Here I am wondering if I'm the

other woman listening to these people talk like you and she are still a thing."

He sighed which meant he was changing the subject, but to her surprise he started to explain.

"I met her at a party in New York last summer. She was beautiful, and sort of reserved for a model, you know. I liked her. She liked to talk and didn't cling to me as if I was a pretty bracelet. I'd fly to meet her or she would fly to meet me when we had time.

God, I don't know how to explain this without sounding like a jerk."

"You've always sounded like a jerk, but one thing led to another and…"

"She asked me if I would marry her."

"So she was desperate. Did you love her? You must have or you wouldn't have said yes."

"Maybe, I don't know, I loved the idea of her. So I bought her a ring, and we told my mom. Oh, she was not happy. She hated her on sight, and Lisette hated Tuscaloosa on sight. She decided then and there we were getting married in France when I flew over to meet her family."

"So what happened in France? Did her daddy take a shotgun to you?"

"No, they welcomed me like a conquering hero. They had a pretty chalet outside Provence. Her parents, a couple of brothers, and a sister all lived there. They were nice enough. Kind of rough around the edges, now that I think about it. No one seemed to work except Lisette. There were signs that something was off but damned if I saw any of them. And then one afternoon about a week before the wedding I walked in on her and her maid of honor, uh … going at it, I guess would be the nice way to put it."

"I thought that was every man's dream. Didn't do it for you, huh, big boy?"

"Shut up, Pepper. It's not funny. She wasn't very good in bed. I thought she was just… I don't know … Christ, you're lying in my arms naked as a fucking jaybird, and I'm talking about sex with someone else. Ouch, don't pinch me. I'm injured."

"Serves you right for keeping things from me. So, Lisette liked girls and not you, is that what I'm getting here? Damn, Jaime, that must have done wonders for your manhood."

"Because I am a first-class stud, I know. I never understood why she'd just lay there until it was over."

"She did the *Harry Met Sally* thing, then?"

"Yeah, she was great at that. Anyway, after I found out her little secret, the other secrets weren't that far behind. The family was living off her, and modeling jobs were getting farther apart. She was afraid of going back to living in the slums in Paris. She thought she'd hook herself a rich, dumb American jock. She had it all planned out. She'd get pregnant and move her girlfriend in with us to take care of her. The girlfriend was supposed to seduce me and…"

"Voila, Tiger Woods all over again."

"Something like that. Needless to say, we

parted ways quietly. She didn't want her dirty little secret to get out, and I, well, I just didn't want it showing up on TMZ."

"So sex with me was rebound sex?"

"Yes. No. I don't know, Cass you drove me crazy with your mouthy ways. The constant bickering, the constantly being around you. I started looking at you like a dying man eyeing a last meal. That day on the patio was unforgivable, but that's when I caved. You don't know how close I came to bending you over and…"

"I get the picture. We'll let it go for now. For what it's worth, I think you are a first-class stud."

"Why thanks, Pepper, and you are far from being a cold fish. Ouch. Stop pinching me. Ouch. Stop it or I'll make you tell me a painful truth about you."

"I don't have any painful secrets."

"Oh yeah, what about those two years you lived in Nashville? I don't know, Cass, that seems an awful lot like a painful man-related secret to me."

"I was going to school. Have you been talking to my mother?"

"You said you taught at a private school in Tennessee for two years. I checked your resume. You were finished with grad school and hadn't started your doctorate yet, so why did you stay after finishing up? Come on, Pepper, I told you mine. You tell me yours."

"I hate you."

"Really? That's not what you said this morning." His voice grew soft, serious as he held his breath again. Damn, those three little words were like ammunition for him.

"So you heard that. I was hoping you hadn't."

"I heard. Let's just say I don't hate you anymore and leave it there for now." She felt tears well in the corners of her eyes. He didn't hate her anymore. What kind of a response was that?

"I had an affair with one of my professors. He said he loved me, and I moved in with him after I graduated. I took the job at a school nearby, and for about a year, everything was great. Sex on Wednesdays and we spent Saturdays in bed. We talked about books and politics, went to the farmer's market on Sunday. We got a dog. Everything was perfect. I contracted for a second year with the school. I liked it there. It wasn't a large school, and the kids were like little sponges. I started having the picket fence fantasy, you know. The house, the dog, the two point four kids who would go to that little school and know all about heirloom tomatoes and…"

"And then what? You walked in on him and another student, didn't you?" She nodded against his chest. The tears became more than just a threat.

"Another aide. She was twenty-two. He said I'd gotten too old and my mind wasn't open to new experiences anymore. I was twenty-four, for fuck's sake. I moved out and she moved in. I stayed the year and finished my contract at the school, then I went home. I never told my mother most of this. She just thinks I had my heart broken. She doesn't know the details."

"But you did have your heart broken, Cass. She probably knows more than you think."

"I know. She's eerie that way. She tried so hard to save me from making the same mistakes she did, and what did I do? Shack up with the first guy to give me a wink. Shit, and now here I am shacked up with you."

"At least you know I'm not banging my student aide."

"It's not funny, Jaime."

"I'm sorry, Cass, I didn't mean to hurt your feelings. It's not as if you waited all this time. You found a rebound guy and…"

"You can shut up now."

"Aw, come on, Cass. Please tell me there's been someone between me and professor douche bag. A cute guy at work, a lonely dad, a lonely mom, the janitor — somebody?" She didn't answer. What was she supposed to say? That she jumped the first guy she saw in the hall after leaving with her tail between her legs. Or one of the guys she grew up with stuck living at home just after she moved back in with her mother. No, thank you.

"Well, okay. That explains some things, I guess. I mean you are very eager to please me and…"

"If you ever want me to please you again, you will drop this topic. I swear, Jaime, just when I think there's a human being hiding under that stupid jock exterior, you have to go and be a jerk again."

"I wouldn't mind exploring that pleasing option, if you are in the mood. Ouch. Cut it out, Pepper. I mean it or…"

"Or you'll what, spank me? Ooh, Jaime, I've been a bad, bad girl and I need a spanking. Think you can catch me with your arm lashed to your body?" She squealed when he locked his left arm around her before she could make a break for it.

"Just because I am half injured doesn't mean I

can't warm your bottom. When I'm done you'll thank me like a good little girl."

"Okay, that just sounds skeevy. And I've got to go pee." She stifled a laugh when he rolled her onto her stomach. His eyes, though ringed with dark circles, burned with that fire that set her blood to bubbling like molten lava. "Are you going to lie there, or are you going to warm my bottom, Lord Ironman?"

"Pepper." His voice turned husky, and it didn't matter if he didn't love her. "You make me crazy."

She gasped when his hand connected with her flesh. "That feels so good, Jaime, do it again." She lifted her rear into the air and wiggled it for him. He laid his head on the small of her back; a strangled groan that sounded oddly like a wounded animal rumbled in his chest. "God, Pepper, you're killing me."

Mercy Celeste

Chapter Twenty-One

On Wednesday, Jaime shanghaied Cass to drive him up to the practice field. Freshly released from total arm immobilization, he wore a sling and seemed more like himself than he had the day before, but he still wasn't ready to drive.

About halfway there, Cass decided there was no reason why Jaime couldn't have driven himself. He was drug-free, mostly pain-free, and full of pent-up energy. He talked all the way, telling her about the guys on the team and the coaches. By the time she followed him onto the field, her hand firmly clutched in his, she decided he'd done this on purpose. She'd never have come otherwise.

"Jay-man, look at you." An overly large man ran past, slapping Jaime on the rear end. "Good to see you aren't dead." Another shouted out.

By the time they reached the fifty-yard line, a small group of men swarmed around them, curiosity about her held in check only by their relief to see him looking and acting like a man not on death's doorstep. They traded banter and relived the night right down to the gory details of Jaime lying on the field before Jaime even seemed to remember he'd dragged her along.

"Hey, Jay-man, aren't you going to introduce the babe?" Another overly large man loomed over her, smiling down at her with a row of gold teeth. "She's sort of short. But I like 'em short."

"And you're overgrown. What did your mother feed you when you were a baby, Miracle Gro?" The words popped out of her mouth before Cass could think to rein in her tongue.

"Pepper, leave the overgrown wide receiver alone. He isn't up to verbal warfare with you. Plus, you really are short."

"I'm five seven, that's hardly short. Just

because you lot ate too many Wheaties as kids doesn't mean there's anything wrong with me."

"Guys this is my friend, Pepper. Pepper, the offensive line."

"Offensive line, huh? Well, that certainly explains a lot."

"Pepper!" His voice dropped an octave, and she knew it was time to shut up before she got hurt, but the biggest one—the one with the gold teeth—started laughing.

"Jay, man, leave her alone. I like her. She's got balls. Hey, Pepper, I got your back, babe." A whistle sounded across the field. He smiled a huge toothy grin, gave her a thumbs-up and ran across the field, the others trailing behind.

"Well, that went better than expected. At least they didn't eat me," she said to a round of laughter, this time from the offensive line coach, Marcus Wells.

"I knew I liked you. Pepper? It's Pepper, right? Hey, Jaime, how are you doing? The doctor told me the arm is progressing nicely. Range of motion looks good, but right now, he wants you to keep it rested. And the ribs look good. Keep it up and I'll put you back out there next Wednesday." He caught Jaime's free hand and pumped it while he talked nonstop.

"Going to do my best, coach."

"I know you, Jay. You're only following doctor's orders because someone is making you. I'm sure it's this lady here. Pepper, you have my sympathies for hooking up with a guy like him. Stubborn, mule-headed … well, you get my drift." He grabbed her hand.

His face split into a wide grin when she blushed. "Look at that. She just put Darnel Johnson in his place, and now she's blushing. She's a keeper, Jay." Jaime didn't say anything to that. He just found her a shaded place to sit, got her a Coke, and went back to pace the sidelines as practice carried on without him. Most often, she found him talking animatedly with a guy about his same build.

"That's my son, Caleb Thompson. He's Jay's backup QB." A woman around her mother's age joined her on the bleachers. "I'm Lucinda Thompson. We met briefly Sunday night."

"I'm sorry. Sunday night is still sort of a blur. I'm Cassandra Pendleton." Cass took her hand noting the curiosity in her eyes. "Everybody, well, everybody except Jaime calls me Cass."

"And what does Jay call you, if not Cass?"

"Pepper. Don't ask; it's a long and confusing story." She settled in to watch the practice, but Lucinda's stare seemed to bore into her.

"Caleb tells me you're the new woman in Jay's life. Seems no one knew the old one was out of the picture. Last thing they heard he was going to marry … what was her name…?"

"Lisette. Yeah, Jaime told me about her. And well, let's just say things didn't work out. But I wouldn't go right to saying I'm his new woman."

"What are you, then, if you don't mind me

asking? I mean Sunday night the two of you looked like a couple even if it was from across the field, and of course, there was that picture splashed all over the internet. You looked pretty cozy in his arms."

"Well, hey, Lucinda, you're sort of putting me on the defensive here. I mean, you're asking some pretty personal questions."

"Well, honey, the guys have been talking, you know, wondering why he's keeping you a secret. But looking at you, I can see that you're not his usual type."

"I'm not supermodel material, I got that. I'm not blonde, I got that too. And I'm not a bimbo, but you know, whatever Jaime and I are or aren't isn't anyone's business but ours."

"No need to get all huffy. I was just curious is all." Lucinda swung one long tan leg over the other and bounced her sandal on her toe. "You seem to have a brain, and honestly, up close you are breathtaking, especially your eyes. I can see

Jay getting confused in those fiery blue orbs of yours. So tell me honey, is he as hot in the sack as he is on the field?"

"Pepper, let's go," Jaime shouted from the field, interrupting the thoughts of mayhem that were currently populating Cass's brain. She could feel her teeth grind together. It was all she could do not to smack the brazen hussy one in the mouth.

"Saved by the bellow." Lucinda smiled, and before Cass could respond, she uncrossed her legs and rose to leave. "Until next time, hon."

* * * * *

"Pepper, sweetheart, would you mind slowing down a bit. You just blew through a red light." Jaime gripped the seat with his one good hand, as she swung hard into a parking lot coming to a halt straddling two spaces. "Uh, Pepper, is something bothering you? Did one of the guys say something to you?"

"It wasn't one of the guys, Jaime. It was a

player's mom." She put the car in park and leaned against the steering wheel, agitation in her every move. "Is it always going to be like this?"

"Like what? What happened exactly, Pepper?"

"Stop calling me Pepper, dammit, Jamie. It's not cute anymore."

"Okay. Cass. What happened?"

"Are we in a relationship or not?"

"I don't know, Cass. Do you want to be?"

"I don't know. I don't, Jaime. I really have no idea what I want, but when people ask, I don't know what to tell them. I mean. Oh yeah sure. Jay Dalton and I are burning up the sheets. God, once he tied me up in New York City and did incredibly dirty things to me, but we're just friends, you know. And I'm tired of my height and hair color being an issue. I haven't heard anything about my weight yet, but I'm sure that's next. I mean, Hell, I know I'm not a bobble-headed lollipop by a long shot. I've got hips and thighs and … and…"

"Cass, will you just slow down? You're not making any sense. Who have you been talking to?"

"Everyone, but today it was your backup's mom, Lucinda Thompson. She said her son Caleb says that the whole team wants to know what happened to your fiancée, and they are all so curious about me. She had the nerve to ask me what you're like in bed. Damn it, Jaime. What do you want from me? Tell me, so I know what to do and say when I'm put in this position next time."

"Wait, back up. You said a woman named Lucinda Thompson said her son Caleb is backup quarterback? For me? Are you sure?"

"Yeah, so? She pointed to the guy you were sort of coaching when she sat down."

"Fuck. Cass, there isn't a guy named Caleb Thompson on the team. That guy is Aaron Havers, and I know for a fact that his mom is in the Bahamas on a second honeymoon with Aaron's dad."

"So who the hell was that Lucinda woman?"

"That is a great question. I'll see if I can find out when we get home. That is, if we get home in one piece."

"Do you want to drive? You can drive if you have a problem with my driving."

"I can't drive a stick right now, baby. You know, doctor's orders." He wiggled the fingers of his right hand just to torment her.

"It's a dual transmission, and right now it's in automatic. You're just being difficult."

"Still, Pepper, the doctor said not to strain my shoulder. You don't want to go against doctor's orders, do you?"

"Fine, but unless shotgun is called on for directions, then shotgun keeps his cakehole shut. I'm getting a milk shake. Do you want a milk shake?" Jaime noticed for the first time that they were sitting in a McDonald's parking lot. "I could stand a chocolate one, if that's all right."

"Fine, two chocolate milk shakes. Anything

else while we're here?"

"A double quarter pounder and some fries, maybe?"

"Okay fine, but you're paying."

"Sure, you'll let me buy you lunch, but you have fits if I try to buy you anything else.

Since you're in a receiving mood, Cass, why don't we go to a jewelry store? You can pick out anything you want. You deserve something pretty after everything you've done for me."

"I don't want jewelry, Jaime. Damn, you just don't get it, do you? I don't want anything from you. I'm not interested in expensive gifts or…"

"Then what do you want, Cass? I mean, I want you to be happy. I will give you the world if you ask me for it. I'll even tell the press you're my girlfriend if it makes you happy. There, Cass. I said you're my girlfriend. Can I buy you a necklace or some earrings or something to celebrate?"

"Is that what you want? Me to be your

girlfriend? Then ask me. Don't tell me."

"Okay, Cassandra Pendleton, will you be my girlfriend?" She sat there looking at him for a long moment, her eyes shimmering with what looked like tears, and then she put the car in gear, drove to the line, and ordered lunch.

Once they were back on the road, he asked her again if she wanted to be his lady.

"Jaime, the last thing I have ever wanted in my entire life was to be your girlfriend." Jaime wisely decided to eat his lunch and just let her drive for a while. Mulling over what was going on just kept leading him back to the land of the confused. So some woman, probably a reporter or blogger, asked Cass a bunch of leading questions under the guise of a common interest. He got that much. If the questions were so upsetting to Cass, then why didn't she just tell the woman where to stick herself? She'd just mouthed off to a six-foot seven-inch giant of a man and lived to tell the tale. She had the balls to take on a nosy bitch.

"If I ask a question, will you take my head off?" He waited until she turned into their neighborhood, hoping she'd cooled down by then. She just looked at him with murder in her eyes. Obviously not, but that wasn't going to stop him from asking. "Are we fighting? I mean I need to know if you're just venting steam or if we're actually fighting, because I can't tell."

"We're always fighting. It's what we do. It's what we've done since kindergarten."

"This feels different. This doesn't feel like the petty arguing we do. This feels oddly... I don't know ... wrong."

"Look, Jaime. We do two things, we fight or we fuck. Since we're not naked, then I guess we're fighting."

"When we get home can we do the other thing you so eloquently mentioned, because I think I'm turned on."

"Sure, Jaime. I'll strip down in the foyer, and we can go at it against the door. I'm sure your mom won't mind, and I'm sure mine is just waiting to catch us in the act. Hell, I'm surprised they didn't come busting in last night."

"Oh, yeah. I forgot about them. Maybe they'll be out shopping or something. I don't want to miss out on make-up sex."

"Don't bet on it, I think they are planning steaks on the grill and probably charades by the pool."

"I need to call in the reinforcements, don't I?"

"As of yesterday."

Chapter Twenty-Two

"They're gone. Can we get naked now?" She was in the middle of a lap when he walked out of the house. "I called up Shontal and got them both emergency full-spa sessions. After that, Franco has been instructed to take them to the ritziest stores he knows. I gave them both a credit card and told them to go crazy. Of course, Franco is under strict orders to call me when they're all shopped out."

"How convenient. Tell me, Mr. Dalton, did my mother put up a fight at being handed into the lap of luxury?" She dove back into the water intending to ignore the needy cat-and-canary look he wore on his egotistical face.

"Unlike her persnickety daughter, Gloria knows a good thing when it's handed to her. I just hope she doesn't go overboard."

"Oh, you just now thought of that, did you? Since she's hooked up with those Red Hats, I don't even know the woman. She takes week-long vacations, runs off to Mississippi for gambling weekends, and has a newfound penchant for male strippers.

What trouble couldn't she get into with unlimited credit?" She laughed at him and swam into the deep end where she knew he wouldn't follow her with his limited mobility. She was right. He just sat on the side of the pool and dangled his feet in, watching her swim with lust-filled eyes. "Stop looking at me like that."

"Like what?" He just grinned, the fire growing brighter as she drew nearer.

"Like you want to eat me."

"But I do want to eat you. I've been hard all afternoon just thinking about what I'm going to do to you once I get you naked."

"And what would that be, precisely?"

"Come out of the water and find out."

"No, thanks. There are sharks up there. I'm safer in here."

"Come on, Pepper. Climb out so we can have our first make-up sex session." His voice turned wheedling, almost pleading, and she almost took pity on him. Almost. "I want to tip you onto that chaise lounge over there and lick your pretty pussy until you come. Then I'm going to let you service me. Then, if you're a really good girl, I'm going to open you wide and slide my cock deep inside you and make you call me God."

"You're not that good." Of course, her nipples chose that moment to go all hard, never mind the molten putty her limbs became. "And besides, who says we are even having sex, especially outside in the open like this."

"I looked everywhere. There isn't a camera within a mile of here at least. No one is in the bushes or up in that oak. No one is on the wall or hiding in the garage. It's just us, Pepper. Don't make me get the jump rope. I left it on the table, just in case you chose to turn obstinate."

Cass couldn't help looking, but the table was just out of sight. The shiver of anticipation was not welcome. "You wouldn't dare."

"I would. I've thought about tying you up and doing all sorts of naughty things to you all afternoon now. But I won't if you come out and play nice with me."

"What if I don't want to?"

"Wouldn't be the first time. Be a good girl, Pepper, and come out of the pool. I promise not to bite."

"I've heard that before, yet the marks speak for themselves. Tell me, Jaime, what did all of your other girlfriends think of your vampiric tendencies?"

"Damn, Pepper, you do know how to kill a good erection. Just for that, I'm not going to have sex with you after all."

"Well, gee goody for me, but you didn't answer the question. And from the rigid set of your jaw I'm not going to like the answer, am I?" She wasn't sure she really wanted to know, but the reckless mood she'd been in all day just would not leave her alone.

"You're the only one, Cass. I've never done that before you. I don't know why I do it. I just … it's hard to describe; sex with you is so intense. I never expect it; it just happens. I try not to use my teeth, but sometimes I just can't help it. I feel this need to…"

"Mark me as yours." She felt lightheaded and heavy all at the same time. "I've seen animals do it."

"I am not an animal. Okay, not always. I've never hurt you, so stop with the mating analogies. I'll stop. There, are you happy? Damn, now I don't want to have sex with you, and I sent the moms off, so there won't be any good food. My day just went to hell."

"I never said I wanted you to stop." Cass swam into the shallow end and up to the steps, where she climbed out. "I just wanted to understand why."

"Well, I can't explain it—not in a way that makes sense anyway. I sort of lose my head and it makes you lose yours. With your body pulsing around me, you take my control away … and that suit looks great on you. Pepper, your nipples are hard as rocks."

"I know; the water is cold. Do you want to suck them?"

"Are we through fighting for today? I'd love to suck your nipples, if you're done trying to emasculate me."

"I thought you wanted to lick my pussy. I love when you lick my pussy, Jaime. I love your tongue down there, hot and wet against my clit. And then when you open me wide and lick inside me, I could come just thinking about it." He smiled that smile of his that said she was in for a world of trouble if she didn't stop playing with fire. Heat throbbed through her body when his lips turned up at the corners. Oh yeah, she was in for it now.

"Pepper, you are a bad girl, aren't you, baby? You tease me and torment me, and you stand there with that body of yours just to see how far you can push me. Tell me you're a bad girl, baby. Tell me what you want me to do to you."

"I want you to lay me down on that chaise over there and suck my titties until I call you God. And then I want you to fill me with your beautiful cock. Jaime, please, I want you to fuck me hard and fast. When I'm done, I want you to bite me and fuck me some more."

"Jesus, Cass, you keep that up, I might just come in my shorts. Slide that suit off, baby, and come over here."

Cass stood for a moment wondering if she'd lost her mind. His eyes turned to golden fire, and she forgot to wonder. She knew she'd lost her mind, and she didn't for one instant care.

Slowly, so slowly, she peeled the straps down her arms, revealing her breasts. The look of intense pleasure on his face drove her past the point of sanity, and within seconds she was standing naked under the blazing Miami sky, her body screaming for something so primal she thought she would burst.

He beckoned to her, and just as she had that day in his office, she left herself behind to do his bidding. Standing in front of him, she let him guide her forward, his eyes looking up at her as he slowly slithered his fingers along her thighs.

"Open for me baby, I want to taste the cream coating your pussy. Spread your legs, Cass. Let me taste you."

God help her, she didn't hesitate. With a wicked smile, he leaned in, and with a flick of his tongue, he had her begging for more.

Somehow, she didn't know how … she found herself on her back on the patio tile crying Jaime's name as he entered her, orgasm taking her beyond the point of caring that they'd forgotten the condom. "Bite me, Jaime. Please, it feels so good when you bite me."

He drove into her in short, frenzied strokes, his breath coming in small gasps. "I love you, Jaime. I love…"

He growled in her ear, she could feel his orgasm start, his thrusts quickened in that way that drove her over the edge. "Bite me," she begged wrapping her arms around his back. She met his thrusts while the world began to spin out of control. His teeth grazed her neck, sinking in just enough to hurt, to bruise. He pinned her hard beneath him until she could only hold on while he poured himself inside her body. Her body quivering around him as she forgot everything she ever knew in her entire life.

Mercy Celeste

Chapter Twenty-Three

Thursday afternoon, Cass slipped on her sunglasses before she walked out of the school into the early afternoon heat and stopped dead in her tracks. She shivered almost as if someone had thrown a bucket of ice down her top; her heart sped up to an alarming rate. She couldn't think.

Flash bulbs went off, someone shoved a camera in her face, then a microphone followed. Five, ten, she couldn't count them all. She didn't understand their shouted questions. Her only thought was flight and getting safely behind iron gates.

In a move she picked up from watching Jaime, she lifted her left arm to protect her chest, and she pushed through the two startled TV starlets and ran for all she was worth to her car. Thank God for automatic locks. She burned rubber pulling out of the lot in her sensible mom wagon. She looked back, noting the sports car one of the doctor's wives drove was blocked in. So much for making assumptions.

It wasn't long before one of the cars caught up with her. She floored it. Picking up her phone, she pressed the first button. Her mom picked up after two rings.

"Open the gates, I'm being chased. Open the gates. I'll be there in thirty seconds."

"What? Honey, what…"

"Open the gates, mom, before I put this car through them."

"Okay, okay. I'm going … I don't know, Jaime. It's Cass. She wants the gates open, something about being chased."

"Just open the gates. I'm turning the corner now." She barely put her foot on the brake as she peeled through the gate, praying that someone had the sense to close it before the first car could follow her inside. She flung the car into park just outside the front door, and without grabbing anything, she bolted to the house just as the front doors opened.

"What's going on, Pepper?" She ran into his arms, holding on while she shook.

"I don't know, ask them." She swung her head at the front gate where as they watched dark sedans and news trucks were pulling up. Flashes going wild as they stood there watching.

"Shit, this can't be good. Did they ask you anything? What did they say?" He pulled her inside just as his phone rang. He ignored it.

"Pictures. That's the only word I caught. I freaked and ran. I didn't know what else to do."

"Pictures? What pictures?" He went pale before he finished speaking; his phone rang again, and this time he went to answer it. "Yeah, Mitch. No, I haven't seen it. Viral? Oh, shit. How bad is it? Well, get an injunction, get it shut down. She's home. The damned jackals caught her leaving school and scared her to death." He punched up his computer typing furiously, and as she watched, he sat down in his chair, nearly missing. "Oh god, damn, fucking, hell, shit, shit. Who is this bitch? Get this down." He hung up, his eyes darting to her. Fear filled them, incapacitating fear that made her knees shake even more than before. "Those pictures?"

"Yeah?"

"Do I want to see?"

"No."

"What pictures?" Her mom said from her side. "What's going on?" She stepped into the room and looked over Jaime's shoulder before Cass could stop her. "Oh, my. That's not good."

"What do we do now?" Cass said quietly; she couldn't stop the shaking in her voice.

"Damage control, and hope like hell Mitch can get an injunction to have the pictures pulled, but..."

"It won't do any good, will it?"

"No, baby, the blog went viral. There's no way to stop it now." A minute later his phone rang again, his face drained of color, he closed his eyes and answered, a look of desperation on his face that nearly broke her heart. "Yes, sir.

Tomorrow morning. I'll be there." He hung up and laid his head on the desk, his hands gripping his knees as he breathed deeply.

"That was my head coach, I have to appear before the commission tomorrow morning to explain or face indefinite suspension. And Cass, they want to talk to you too. Early."

The phone rang again, and he answered it. There was pain and fear in his voice, but Cass couldn't go to him. She felt drained of everything; her limbs were heavy, her heart thudded painfully in her chest, and she couldn't breathe. She could only stand and stare as her whole world exploded around her.

"Come on, honey. Let's get you something to drink. A Coke, maybe the caffeine will help."

"Vodka. You can add Coke if you want. Just find the damned vodka." She let her mom drag her into the kitchen where Jaime's mom smiled happily at them from behind the stove. Something sweet and savory reached her nose. Before Helen could say a word, Cass rushed past her to the sink, her lunch no longer a lump in her stomach.

"What's going on? Cass, are you okay, honey?" Her voice was too sweet too expectant, and Cass couldn't answer. She retched again, her arms shaking so badly she could barely hold herself up. "Morning sickness?"

"It's not fucking morning sickness. I'm not pregnant. I'm … it's all ruined. Everything is ruined. No one will hire me now, I won't be allowed back at the Boys and Girls Club. I'm ruined." She sank to the floor, but not before she saw Jaime standing in the doorway. "And so is he. Over some Goddamned dirty pictures of us that shouldn't even exist. It's all ruined."

"I'll be damned if I'm going to let this ruin

either one of us, Cass. Detective Ryan, Mitch, and even Sam are on their way. The cops are already clearing the street. It'll all be fine, you'll see."

"For you, maybe. You're a jock. You're supposed to misbehave—boys will be boys and all that shit. What about me? There are pictures of me wearing nothing but..." She shook her head, noticing the stunned look on her mom's face, the same one mirrored on Jaime's mom. "Stop looking at me like that. I didn't want any of this. I liked being anonymous. I don't want to be some ... some football-groupie-sex-toy. Now look at me, I'm infamous or notorious or whatever you want to call it. Whatever you do, Jaime, just remember that genie is not fitting back into the bottle. No school system in the country will ever hire me again. I am ruined permanently."

"I'm sorry, baby." Was all he said before she heard him walk away.

"Where is that vodka?" She looked up at the two women passing secret meaningful glances.

"And there better not be any tranquilizers in it. I'll kick both of you in the ass if you try to slip me something. I don't care whose mom you are."

* * * * *

Functioning on very little sleep, Jaime paced the hallway waiting for the commissioner's panel to finish questioning Cass. After she'd calmed down, after a glass or two of liquid courage that didn't stay inside her, and after the cavalry arrived, the game plan for the day took shape.

Armed with photos of his property, the blackmail letters, and all of the packets of damning photographs along with Detective Ryan's stalled investigation, Mitch was able to mount a defense that should save Jaime's job. Public opinion was another matter altogether, but that was for a later date.

The blogger, LuSINda Cummings—God, what a monster—gave testimony as well.

Under extreme duress, she admitted that she received the photos from a woman claiming to be

Jaime's jilted fiancée. She admitted the sneak attack on Cass the day before, and naturally assumed that Lisette was the jilted fiancée when she wrote her scathing "cheating scumbag" story about Jaime, going so far as to call Cass a whore for taking his money while she was screwing him. She published the bondage photos as proof of Jaime's philandering ways. Never mind that he and Lisette had parted ways months before that happened.

Mitch had been unsuccessful in reaching Lisette, which left Jaime to wonder why she would have gone to such lengths to punish him. Especially when he could ruin her if he chose to retaliate. Why find a nasty skank Perez Hilton wanna-be? Why blackmail him? Why didn't she just ask him for the money outright? There were too many whys and too many lies.

When Cass stepped out of the office, she looked shaky but she held her head high, and color had returned to her cheeks. She looked lovely in a white skirt and blue silk blouse that set off her eyes, another pair of killer ankle-wrap shoes on her feet, these in navy blue. She left her hair down, and he wanted to run his hands through it, pull her into his arms, and just hold her until it was all better. But he knew she wasn't ready for that yet.

"How'd it go?" He settled for taking her hand while they waited for a verdict.

"Fine. They asked me a lot of questions about, well, everything. How I came to be employed by you. How long we've known each other. If I knew about the photos. I told them the truth about everything. About all those years of fighting with you and that we were both surprised to find ourselves attracted to each other. I told them I'd never met Lisette, and to my knowledge, she had not attempted to contact you. Why is this so important anyway? They can't make the pictures go away. They can't stop the scandal that's escalating outside this room. They can't give me my dignity back."

"I know, Cass. I'm sorry, but as horrible and selfish a thing it is to admit, the first step is to make sure I am cleared of any wrongdoing. Sexual misconduct isn't tolerated in the league anymore. I know that sucks. I'm sorry, but that's the way it is. I've already filed defamation charges against that Lusinda creature, and if we find Lisette, I'll ... I'll wring her neck. Then all we can do is hope it goes quietly away."

"But Jaime, what if..."

She stopped talking when the coaches and commission representatives walked out of the room. Her hand gripped his tightly as they waited.

"We're going to turn this matter over to the proper authorities; stalking and harassment does not fall within our purview." A gray-haired man with a strong grip shook Jaime's hand. "We trust this will go away as quickly as possible."

"We can only try, sir." He made himself

remain cordial, but his nerves were to the point of fraying beyond his control.

"Jay, we hate to do this, but the press is waiting. We want to get a blanket on this fire as quickly as possible. I'm sorry, but this is the only way. Just tell the truth—this was a consensual, private matter, and Miss Cummings clearly has a vendetta. We're all here for you. The coaches, the team, everyone is outside." Marcus Wells came to his side, his hand on his shoulder giving him comfort.

"Okay, Coach." He cringed inside. He didn't mind talking about the game in interviews but this—this was too personal, too close to home. He squeezed Cass's hand.

"Are you up to this, Pepper? You can stay here if you want to."

"No, I'll come. I might pass out or puke during it, but I'll be right there with you." The smile she wore was tight. He could see her pulse racing at the base of her neck. She looked as frightened as he felt.

"Well, okay then, let's get this over with."

They stepped out into the bright sun-covered field. Jaime shielded his eyes as he looked over the crowd assembled in the fan area. Cameras, microphones, mini recorders—every sort of device he'd ever seen, trained right on him and then onto Cass.

She held her head up and walked with him, holding his hand for comfort. Just as he stepped up to the podium loaded with microphones, she squeezed his hand before letting him go.

"Well, I guess you all know why we're here today. So I'll skip right to the good part if you don't mind." He cleared his throat, feeling sweat break out on his upper lip.

"Lusinda Cummings alleged on her blog that I am cheating on my supposed fiancée with Cassandra Pendleton. The truth is, Lisette and I split in the early spring. We discovered that we had nothing in common. To my knowledge, she is still in Europe, and I've had no contact with her since April before Cass came back into my life.

"The photos that Miss Cummings posted on her blog were offensive and damaging.

Alluring and titillating, too. I guess." There were some snickers in the crowd. He ignored them. "But the fact of the matter is those photos were taken of me and Miss Pendleton without our consent or knowledge. All of the photos, and yes, there are many more than what Miss Cummings posted, were taken while we were alone in the privacy of our home. Some of the photos were shot through windows with telescopic lenses. There are others of Cass and me sleeping in our bed. These photos should not exist. The person who took these photos came onto our property without our permission and violated our privacy. And now, whoever this person is, who is using Miss Cummings as a mouthpiece for his or her vile agenda, has posted our most intimate moments for the titillation of the Internet and to harm my and Miss Pendleton's reputations and our careers.

"I will not apologize for what I do in the privacy of my home. I have only one thing to ask you to consider before I take Miss Pendleton home so we can try to put our lives back on track. If someone were secretly filming you in your bedroom, what would the world see? Think about that before you judge us."

People started shouting questions, but Jaime wasn't going to answer questions. He reached for Cass's hand and started to lead her away from the podium when a voice shrieked over the others.

"Liar. You are a liar, Jaime Dalton." The speaker dropped the J sound in his name, replacing it with the H sound, and to his knowledge, only one other person in Miami had ever called him Jaime.

"Alicia? What are you doing here?"

"You brought that whore into our home. *Our* home. You brought her right in the front door, and you kicked me out on the street. I begged you not to bring her home. I begged you not to hire her, and what did you do? You made me carry that whore's luggage into my room. You gave that whore my room, and you tossed me aside like garbage. Oh yeah, whore, you better look scared — you took my room, my man, my life. I owe you big time." Alicia slurred the words, stumbling over them as she pushed her way through the crowd, seemingly oblivious to the cameras recording every word out of her deranged mouth. Her accent slipped, becoming rougher, more guttural the longer she ranted.

Jaime stepped in front of Cass, hoping to keep her out of the line of sight of the woman who, as he watched, reached into her handbag and pulled out a small handgun.

"Alicia, be reasonable. You didn't live in my house; you were just my cook. We weren't in a relationship. And … and Cass has nothing to do with you. She…"

"Oh baby, we were so in love, right up until you went away to Paris with that ... that *puta*. She tricked you into loving her, and when you came home, you didn't even have the decency to break my heart in private. You paraded your whore under my nose saying she was your ... what did you call her? Your Girl Friday. Yeah, that was it. I knew just as soon as my back was turned that you'd be screwing her."

"You threw a sugar bowl at my head. I fired you, Alicia. There was never anything between us. I paid you to cook my meals."

"It's a pity I missed your head. But with this, I'm not going to miss. I sent those pictures as a warning. You didn't take my warning, and now you and your slut are going to pay."

Jaime didn't think he took a step off the podium. He made eye contact with two of his men, who pushed through the reporters who were just standing there in stunned silence while this whole thing played out. He hit the ground running, just as Darnel Johnson hit her from behind.

Time seemed to play funny things with his head. He saw the gun flash just before it flew from her hands, the retort coming a second later. He stopped dead in his tracks. Darnel had the laughing woman on the ground, holding her, his eyes looking past Jaime, horror filling their dark depths.

Jaime spun in the air, taking two steps back to the podium only to stop again as Cass's eyes met his. She stood there, shock clear on her face, her hand on her hip, and for a moment he felt relief wash over him. If it weren't for the dark stain that oozed from between her fingers, marring the white of her skirt as it traced its way ever downward he would have thought she was fine.

"*Pepper!*" He didn't know how he made it to her before her knees gave out. "Pepper. No, Pepper. No, baby. Stay with me, Pepper. Look at me … Cass. Cassandra, look at me." She smiled, her eyes focused on him when she laid her hand on his cheek.

"I see you, Jaime. It's all over, isn't it?"

"No, baby. It's not over. Cass, Pepper, don't … I need help here. Cass, baby. Stay with me, Cass."

"I love you, Jaime." Her smile turned wan, her eyes unfocused.

"I love you, Cass. Cass!" A pair of large arms locked around his chest, lifting him away from her just as her eyes closed. "Let me go. Cass!"

"*Cass. Pepper.* Oh my God, what have I done?"

Mercy Celeste

Chapter Twenty-Four

"Alicia Gonzalez died in a car accident in Texas five years ago." Detective Ryan sat down beside him in the waiting room, his voice grim.

"So who the hell was that woman who almost killed Pepper?" Jaime glanced out the window at the setting sun as he bounced his legs, his hands balled into fists he couldn't seem to unclench.

"Her name is Yolanda Gray. She's thirty-five years old and from New Jersey. She's wanted in New Jersey and New York for multiple counts of fraud and identity theft among other things. She assumed Alicia Gonzalez's identity nearly four years ago. The temp agency that sent her to you is scrambling to find out how she slipped through their vetting process. And hoping like hell that you don't sue them." Ryan spoke softly, but every eye in the room was focused on them. "And that's not the worst of it."

"How can there be anything worse? Some delusional lunatic tried to kill Pepper. I want her buried. I want her head on a pike. I want…"

"Just listen, Jay. We are doing everything we can, but right now, it is starting to look like she really is a lunatic and is trying for an insanity plea. But Jay, the woman's crimes against you and Pepper go much deeper than just the picture scam."

"What do you mean? What else could she have possibly done?"

"She's been living in your house for years. When you were gone, she lived there openly, coming and going as if she owned the place. When you were in residence, she parked down the street and slipped in through the back gate, climbed the trellis to the bedroom you and Cass share. She was sleeping in the house with you, and you never knew. After you fired her and changed the security codes, she found another way in. She's been in the house with you and Cass. She's been there alone with Cass. She could have hurt her at any time. And there are more pictures, some taken just a couple of days ago, out by the pool."

"Fuck, fuck, fuck. Cass kept talking about things out of order. Paint cans moved around, the kitchen rearranged. I didn't listen to her. I thought she was just looking for something to argue about. Alicia or whatever her name is was messing with her. Shit. Fuck. What else? There's more, isn't there?"

"Cam Cameron opened his books to us. He didn't want to. We had to get a warrant to search your financials through Cameron's firm. Yolanda has been slowly cleaning you out. She stole a set of checks and opened a credit card in your name. She convinced Cameron that she was your fiancée and that you gave her access to the account. He didn't bat an eye until you called him ready to kick his ass. He's been hiding since then."

"There was nearly two million dollars in that account. She couldn't have gotten it all in a couple of months."

"She wrote elaborate checks to her multiple identities. Fifty thousand here. A hundred there. Oh and congratulations, it seems you own the house next door now as well. She paid a million for it, so you got it for a steal. She bought it the week after you fired her. She was very adept at acting as your legal representative, had the law lingo down pat. She can sign your name better than you can." At this point Jaime was beyond caring; he just hitched his shoulders. "Should I press charges against Cameron? How much can be recouped at this point?"

"That's entirely up to you. She duped him and he's ashamed, that's for sure. At this point, whatever property you can prove she bought with your money is about all you're going to get back. The house is already in your name. I think the car could be proven. An unemployed woman buying a car with cash, it shouldn't be that hard.

Anything from the credit card. Cameron will have those bills. After that, it's going to be up to a judge. Look, man, I know right now that you aren't really processing all this. I'll just tell you that we have her on so many charges that she will never get out of prison. Trespassing, theft, fraud, stalking, harassment, attempted murder…"

He stopped speaking when the door into the ER opened and the surgeon stepped out, his face grim. He spoke to Gloria, but Jaime could hear every word. "She's going to be fine. The bullet missed any vital organs. There was extensive tissue damage complicated by blood loss, but she is stable and will pull through. Though the baby, I'm afraid, wasn't so lucky. If we'd known, maybe we could have prevented spontaneous abortion, but well, there's no way to know now."

"Cass was pregnant?" he said; the floor seemed to be shaking beneath him.

The surgeon nodded. "About six weeks along.

I'm sorry for your loss."

"I'll add murder of an unborn child to the charges," Ryan said as he turned to leave his face gone cold.

"No." Jaime grabbed his arm. "I don't want her going through that if she didn't know. At least spare Cass that much; she's been through enough."

"All right, unless Cass chooses to add the charges later."

"That will be up to her. I don't want the media knowing about this," he said to the room at large. "This is private. No one needs to know we lost a baby in this mess." Jaime watched as his extended family, his coach, his teammates, his mother, and Cass's mother all nodded in agreement, and then he went and collapsed into a chair.

* * * *

"Jaime?" Her tongue felt heavy, almost as if she'd had nothing to drink for days.

"Cass, honey. You're awake?" It wasn't Jaime

who answered.

"Did you give me a tranquilizer, Mom? I told you to stop doing that." Her mother's hand was warm against her cheek. "Are we in the hospital? Is Jaime all right? I thought his arm was healing?"

"Honey, Jaime is fine."

"Then why is he just lying over there? Is that blood on his shirt? Why is Jaime covered in blood?" He lay so still in the bed not far away. She tried to go to him, but the tubes connecting her to the annoying blipping machines wouldn't let her. "That's my blood, isn't it? I remember something…"

"We had to slip him a Mickey for his own good. He was starting to wear a hole in the floor. He wouldn't eat. He wouldn't leave your side."

"How long have I been asleep? I hurt all over. My side feels like it's on fire." A flash of light shot across her memory. The laughing woman. Jaime's horrified eyes. Red paint. She'd spilled paint on her skirt. "She shot me. Mom, that woman shot me."

"Yesterday morning. You've been in and out of consciousness for nearly forty hours. But you're going to be fine." Her mother squeezed her hand in hers there was something in her eyes—a sadness that didn't make sense.

"What aren't you telling me? Did someone die? That wide retriever—what was his name? Did she shoot him, too? I saw him jump for her, and then … I don't remember anything after that. Jaime? She was going to kill me, wasn't she, because of Jaime?"

"Honey, why didn't you tell Jaime you were pregnant?" Her mother's voice trembled.

"I'm not pregnant. Why do you and Helen keep thinking that? Were pregnant? What do you mean were?"

"You didn't know? Oh Cass, honey, I'm so sorry."

"I was pregnant. She shot my baby? That bitch shot my baby? I … will I be able to have children?"

"It was the stress of the surgery, Cass. You miscarried. The doctors say there is no damage to your uterus. You can have more children. You and Jaime…"

"I don't want to have children with Jaime. I want to go home, Mom. Please, I want to go back to Alabama. Jaime doesn't love me. He just likes to … I'll get pregnant again if I stay. He's persistent. He wears me down until I give in, and he doesn't love me."

"Honey, Jaime loves you. He just doesn't know how to tell you how he feels."

"Even if he does, there will still be women, lots of women. Maybe the next one will finish what the last one started. I can't keep doing this. I can't keep worrying about him getting hurt. He nearly broke his neck last week. I can't stand the constant fighting anymore. It tears me down to think all he wants from me is sex. He got me pregnant, and because of him I lost the baby."

"Honey, think about what you're saying. It wasn't Jaime's fault that woman had a screw loose."

"I want to go home, Mama. Please, take me home. I can't stay here anymore. I can't stand the heartbreak."

"Okay, baby. As soon as the doctors say you can fly, I'll take you home."

* * * * *

The anguish in her voice tore him apart. She was right. If she stayed, she would end up having his child. If she stayed, he would end up losing everything to her. If she stayed … he rolled away, letting the drug pull him back under … if she stayed his heart wouldn't break into a million little pieces.

Chapter Twenty-Five

The first weekend of October came before Cass was ready. Summer had somehow slipped away at the end of September. There was a chill in the air after sunset now.

Cass went about her days much the same as she had before her brief time in Miami.

Putting out applications and trying to keep herself busy. The ongoing scandal had cost her friends. Some of the women who once welcomed her now turned their backs on her when they saw her coming. Her Sunday school teacher even took her aside to read her the riot act for her many and varied sins.

The largest sin apparently was wrecking the favored son's chances at a championship season. Miami had lost all of their last three games, though the first two were because Jaime was on the sidelines instead of playing. His backup had tried valiantly, and both games they'd almost, almost won. Cass didn't watch the games. She didn't want to see him kill himself. He hadn't called her before any of the games either.

She'd waited, watching the phone, but it never rang. She didn't know if she felt disappointed or relieved.

She learned of Yolanda Gray or Alicia Gonzalez, or whatever her name was on the news. A wanted felon in two states. She'd been declared unfit to stand trial for attempting to kill her. Jaime looked tired and pale in the courtroom the day she was taken away to a mental facility in North Florida. New York and New Jersey were filing extradition papers, but for now, she was staying put in Florida.

Gloria and Helen came home with her, and both went back to work. Her mother begged her to stop lying around moping on the sofa the few days a week she allowed herself to lie around moping. However, after the verbal sin-lashing she'd gotten, she found herself lying on the couch in her robe more than she cared to admit.

On Saturday that first week of October, Cass was again lying on the couch watching television trying to avoid sports, news, sports news, Hallmark commercials, anything on the Lifetime network, and diaper commercials, which pretty much left her with just the Weather Channel for company. Even they liked to torment her with shots of the beautiful weather Miami was having this weekend.

The doorbell rang just as she decided she should turn off the television and get a life.

She opened the door to find the FedEx guy standing there holding an envelope. Her heart started racing, and she knew she must have looked like she was about to drop because the guy asked her if she was okay. She assured him she had never been better and took the package from him.

It was for her, the return address one she didn't know in Miami. She set it on the table as if it were a bomb and fixed herself a sandwich, took a bite of the sandwich, and tossed it in the trash because it tasted like sawdust. Everything tasted like sawdust. She ate when her mother forced her to. She wasn't starving.

She gulped milk, pouring half a bottle of chocolate syrup into it, trying not to remember the milk shakes she and Jaime had the day before their lives went to hell.

Chocolate milk was the only thing that stayed down. Sometimes toast. Except toast tasted like sawdust with jelly on it.

She went to her room. The dolls on the shelf looked at her with their dead baby eyes, so she went back to the couch. A while later, she found herself circling the envelope like a vulture. It hadn't exploded.

Maybe it would have been better if it had.

She picked it up, and closing her eyes, she ripped the tab and dumped the contents onto the table. Dirty pictures wouldn't make a clattering noise would they? She peeked with one eye and saw the mirror side of what looked like a CD shining up at her. She looked in the envelope and found a single sheet of paper trapped beneath the flap.

I thought this might help you.

That was all it said; there was no signature. "Help me with what?" She picked up the disc and found the words *Watch Me* scrawled on it in the same handwriting. It was a DVD.

Shaking, she held the thing out at arm's length as she walked back to the living room. She hesitated but finally loaded it into the machine. The scene switched from a sunny day in Miami to a different sunny day in Miami. The one in which her world had literally almost come to an end.

Instead of the one-minute clip of that day she'd seen on the news, the scene that played out before her was horrific, detailed, heartbreaking.

The woman Alicia, confronting Jaime with her delusional lies. The disbelief on Jamie's face that turned to stark fear. He stepped in front of her, shielding her. She saw him look past Alicia, his eyes sending some sort of message, and then he jumped from the podium, rushing the gun. But they were too late. Alicia squeezed the trigger, aiming past Jaime. Then she hit the ground, laughing maniacally as a group of men restrained her.

She saw herself standing there, fear holding her to the spot. Her body jolted with the impact of the bullet, and all she did was reach up with her hand and cover the spot. Cass remembered that. There wasn't much pain, just a burning sensation, followed by wet sticky blood.

Jaime caught her before she collapsed, and she reached for his face, smearing him with blood. His panicked cries for help and for her to look at him turned to, "I love you, Cass. Look at me, Cass.

Pepper."

It took six full-size football players to pull him away from her so the team medics could help her. It took more than six to restrain him after they pulled him away. He was like a man on fire. Then he just dropped to his knees. She could see tears, as he mouthed,

"No, baby. No, baby. Don't leave me." Then the footage ended.

She turned off the player and lay on the couch, holding her ribs. That day at the airport, he'd kissed her on her forehead and watched her fly away. He didn't say anything then about loving her. He hadn't begged her to stay. He'd simply said good-bye. Then she was gone. Why hadn't he begged her to stay?

"Why didn't you tell me you loved me? Why did you let me go?" she screamed at the television. "I hate you, Jaime Dalton. I HATE YOU."

* * * * *

"Do you have the game on?" His voice over the

phone sounded tired.

"No." But she did. After watching the DVD repeatedly until she finally broke, she needed to see him for real.

"Don't lie to me, Pepper. I know you have it on." She could hear the crowd around him, his breath as he waited for her to answer.

"Why are you breathing heavy? And stop calling me Pepper."

"Because I'm tired, I'm out of shape, and its cold out here." She noticed the steam coming from the breath of the guy currently on camera.

"Where are you?"

"New York. Are you home alone?"

"We're not having phone sex, so stop thinking about it."

"I wasn't. I wasn't—stop making that noise."

"What noise? I didn't make a noise."

"You do this sort of catchy sound in your throat when you don't like something I say. Sort of between a humph and a croak."

"I do not sound like a frog, Jaime Dalton. Go play your violent game of tag and leave me alone."

"Pepper, come home. I need you, baby, please."

"No, Jaime, don't ask me that, not now."

"Am I on TV?"

"No, they've got that big guy on right now. I can't remember his name, the one with gold teeth."

She heard him shout something, and then the camera swung around to him. His arm beckoning the guy to come closer. "Hey, are you live?" She saw him as well as heard him. His face looked gaunt. He looked as tired as he claimed to be.

"Yeah!" she heard the cameraman shout back.

"Good. Come here. I've got something I need to tell someone, and she isn't listening."

She could hear the commentators wondering what was going on over the airwaves and got a sick feeling in the pit of her stomach.

"Cass. Look at me. Listen to me. I love you. I've always loved you. I fell in love with you on August 18, 1986. I pulled your hair at recess, and you knocked me flat on my ass." She heard him over the phone, his mouth moving to the words on television, and then she heard him in stereo.

"Don't do this, Jaime. Not like this. Please."

"I let you go because I loved you, and I didn't want you to be hurt any more than you already were. It was a mistake. Come home to me, baby. Cassandra. Come home. I won't call you Pepper ever again. I promise to stop fighting with you. I promise…"

"Jaime. We lost a baby … we didn't even know it existed, and I can't stop grieving for it. I'm not ready to think about…"

"Cass, we'll make more babies. I want babies, the two point four you want, and we'll get a dog. We can't start working on those babies with you gone. Come home, baby?"

"No, Jaime. Why don't you understand it's not

about children? It's about you making me crazy. It's about you risking your neck. It's about…"

"I'll quit. I'll quit right now, I'll walk off the field right now, Cass. I'll go to medical school. Football doesn't mean a thing to me anymore. I'll set this helmet down and walk out right now. Just say you're coming home, and I'm gone."

"Are you crazy?" Somehow, she could hear a little tinny version of her own voice coming from the television. "If you walk off that field, you'll blame me for the rest of your life. I won't let you throw away something you love just because…"

"Just because what? You were going to say you love me, weren't you?"

"No, I was going to say I'd become the most hated person in Miami, and probably the whole the country. Jaime, we aren't meant to be. Just let me go."

"No, I won't let you go. I gave you time to heal. Now it's time to put your life back together, to put our lives back together. If there is one thing football has taught me, it's never to give up on something you want. And, Cass, I want you. You're all I've ever wanted. You and your sassy back-talking mouth. You're the only person who can knock me on my ass. You've been doing it since the first day of kindergarten."

"Jaime, no…"

"Marry me. I want you to be my wife. I need you to be my wife."

"Jaime…"

"Or, I'm good just living in sin, just so long as it's in the same house. Cassandra Pendleton—" He got down on his knee, the camera following him, and that's when the dam broke.

"Jaime, please don't…" She could hear own sobbing voice over the television.

"Cassandra Pendleton, I'm coming to get you tomorrow morning, and we're going to Vegas and getting married."

"I've told you before about telling me what to do. If you want something ask for it, don't tell."

"Marry me, Cass? Please, baby. I'm broken and begging. Please, Cassandra Pendleton, will you be my wife?"

She couldn't do anything for the tears clogging her throat. She heard the sniffled sob and the rush of breath as she tried to stop the flood.

"Only if you call me Pepper."

"Hey, Pepper, don't bother packing for Vegas. You aren't going to need any clothes."

Then he gave his phone to the cameraman and ran off and showed New York what a tropical storm was all about.

Mercy Celeste

Chapter Twenty-Six

She was waiting for him when he walked in her front door the next morning. She looked frail and fragile with puffy swollen eyes ringed by dark circles. She was a sight for sore eyes and then some.

"Hey ya, Pepper. Are you ready to go?" He felt his heart skip a beat waiting for her to answer. All night he'd second-guessed his actions. Putting her on the spot like that had been a spur of the moment decision. Despite the fact that he was once again the focus of an overly curious media, he would do it again, if it got her to come home.

She fell into his arms, her whole body trembling like a leaf. "What took you so long? I've been ready for hours."

"Well, then, grab your gear and let's go."

She grabbed her purse and walked out of the house on his arm to the waiting limo.

He'd hired a private jet to take them to the bright lights of Vegas. The flight had been excruciating. He wanted her, but it wasn't time yet. She was still fragile, and sex would just complicate things.

He checked his watch at the hotel, setting it for Vegas time. "Hey, Pepper, I've been thinking. You might need a dress or something before we head off to the chapel so why don't I leave you in the boutique to pick something out while I go check on our reservations."

"Don't you dare leave me here, Jaime Dalton." She turned those smoky blue eyes on him, and for the first time in weeks, he felt as if everything was right with his world. "I will never forgive you if you desert me right now." She stopped talking when a trio of people walked out of the store, her eyes going wide with surprise. "Have I told you lately how much I hate you?"

"Not in a long, long time. Welcome back, Pepper. Now go let the moms and Shontal do what they have to do to make you look less like a gothic club kid and more like a bride. I'll see you later. Oh, and Pepper, behave."

"Bite me."

"Maybe tonight if you are a really good girl. Of course, I do miss the bad Pepper."

"Jaime, remind me to kill you later."

* * * * *

The dress wasn't some off-the-rack cocktail dress but a full-scale lace and satin gown that cinched in her waist and lifted her breasts to unbelievable heights. The lace panel that covered her bosom and wrapped around her neck was the only thing keeping the dress on this side of tasteful.   Shontal tsked and scolded, as he set to work on her hair, clipping, curling, and fussing until she thought he was going to pull her bald. The hotel spa provided the rest of the services, and when she was finished she looked like a fairy princess instead of the half-starved waif she'd been a couple of hours earlier.

Her mother stepped from the fitting room in a beautiful coral dress that befitted the mother of the bride, just as Jaime's mom stepped out in an aqua number that had both herself and Shontal howling. The moms just gave them a go-to-hell look and didn't listen to their taunts about team colors and doing it on purpose.

Then, almost as if there was a preset time and as if they'd all been plotting behind her back, Shontal pushed her to a set of doors. "Oh, wait, honey, here. You're forgetting this." He shoved a bouquet of coral, aqua, and cream flowers into her hand just as her mom took her arm and all but dragged her through the doors.

She stopped inside, her breath caught at the sight before her. A full-scale chapel, decked out in flowers and silk ribbons, filled with people she knew, lots of people she knew. An entire football team sat on one side, except for Darnel Johnson.

He sat on the other side with Mrs. Perkins from next door, who was beaming as if she'd just won the lottery and a date with Sean Connery at the same time.

Her cousins, his cousins, friends from home, friends from Miami. And up at the podium stood Jaime, in black tux and coral tie. He looked scared to death.

The first strains of the wedding march came from a string quartet, and her mom tugged her gently down the aisle and placed her hand in Jaime's.

When it was all over, she looked at the simple band of diamonds he placed on her finger, choking back a sob. She kissed the groom, and before she could even think of a thing to say, she found herself flying over Jaime's shoulder. "Put me down, you jerk."

"Hush, Pepper, you are making a scene." She heard the laughter in his voice as he laid his hand across her rear end. "Thank you all for coming.

Enjoy the reception and don't lose too much at the slots and go see a show or three. Pepper and I have some unfinished business, and we'll see all of you. Later, hopefully before you all go home; but if we don't, then thank you again for sharing our happiness with us, and okay, bye now."

He moved quickly down the aisle, and she could see shocked faces following their quick escape. Cass starting laughing and couldn't stop. Before he made it through the doors, she remembered something. "Jaime, stop. The bouquet. We need to throw the bouquet."

She could hear the frustration in his voice, but he stopped. "Okay, just make it quick, will you, Pepper?"

Cass waited a moment before she reached up and chucked the flowers into the air.

Shontal hooted as he held it over his head. "Honey, thank you, and don't do anything I wouldn't do," he shouted to hoots of laughter. Then Jaime dropped her to her feet just inside the elevator and punched the penthouse button.

"How do I get you out of this dress?" His lips touched hers consuming her as he fumbled with the neck until he found the hooks. She sighed when his hands cupped her breasts. "Never mind. I figured it out."

"Jaime, that feels so good. Do it again." He pinched her nipples between his fingers.

Her body became magma. "I missed you."

"I know you did, baby."

"I want to come for you. Jaime, make me come, right here in the elevator."

"There might be cameras."

"I don't care."

She heard him groan as he tugged her dress down her body, skimming her legs with his rough hands. "I love your pink panties, Pepper, but right now, they've got to go, baby."

"Then get rid of them. Please, I need you inside me. Now, Jaime. I'm going to explode if you don't … oh God, that feels good." She stepped out of her panties and leaned against the elevator wall as Jaime touched her clit with his tongue.

"Come for me, baby." He slipped a finger inside her as he rose to his feet, nipping her nipples on the way to capture her lips. "Purr for me, baby. Oh yeah, that's a good girl."

Using quick, hard strokes he had her trembling before the doors whooshed open. She cried out his name just as he lifted her out of her dress puddle and set her on her strappy-heeled feet in the middle of a posh room, her body still quaking from orgasm.

"Ready for seconds?" He had her on the floor before the elevator doors swooshed closed with a ding.

"Oh yeah, and thirds." He filled her in one thrust. She wrapped her arms around his shoulders, the material of his jacket soft against her skin. "I love you, Jaime Dalton."

"Took you long enough to realize it." He smiled down at her, his eyes going all fiery, his breath all soft. "I love you too, Cassandra Pendleton."

"Pepper Dalton. My name is Pepper Dalton now."

"So what's my new name?"

"Lord and Master Ironman. Oh God, do that again."

He flexed inside her, taking his time. He smiled down at her as her body started to quiver around him. "I like that. Call me God again, and I'll make you come, Pepper Dalton."

"More, God, please more."

"That's more like it." He thrust into her, gliding in fast, hard thrusts until she called him God and every other deity she could think of. When she thought she couldn't stand another minute, his teeth grazed her neck, and she cried out for more.

Mercy Celeste

About Mercy Celeste

Mercy Celeste is the pen name and super hero persona of mild mannered MJ Colbert....which is bull, I'm not mild mannered. I was, in fact, raised in a barn--or several. We even had grain silos. My motto growing up, anything a boy can do, I'm right behind him doing it just as well or better. I've broken too many bones to begin to count. Scraped, skinned or scarred pretty much everything that can be scraped, skinned or scarred. How I'm still walking and talking is a miracle.

So about the writing, well, I don't really consider myself to be a writer. I'm a storyteller, and when I have a story to tell, it won't rest until it's twisted me up and purged itself. The result is at times comical or tragic, depending on the people who live in my head and what they have to say. Most days that's not a lot of anything. Others I can't shut them up. They especially love when I'm driving, oh, yeah, a drive across town is a lesson in how not to get myself killed or be pulled over for reckless driving. And those are the good days.

Welcome to my crazy world, if it's boring now, wait five minutes, and don't blink. Things have a tendency to get interesting around me.

Mercy Celeste

Other Books by Mercy Celeste

Available from Liquid Silver Books
Let it Go

Available from Total E Bound Books
Behind Iron Lace
Under a Crescent Moon

Available from MJC Press
The 51st Thursday
In from the Cold (book one in The Cold Series)
Beyond Complicated
Six Ways from Sunday (book one in the Southern Scrimmage series)
Sidelined (book two in the Southern Scrimmage series)
Offside Chance (book three in the Southern Scrimmage series)
Two Point Conversion
Crazy from the Heat

Printed in Great Britain
by Amazon.co.uk, Ltd.,
Marston Gate.